HORRID HENRY'S Halloween Horrors

Francesca Simon spent her childhood on the beach in California, and then went to Yale and Oxford Universities to study medieval history and literature. She now lives in London with her family. She has written over 50 books and won the Children's Book of the Year at the Galaxy British Book Awards for *Horrid Henry and the Abominable Snowman*.

Tony Ross is one of the most popular and successful of all children's illustrators, with almost 50 picture books to his name. He has also produced line drawings for many fiction titles, for authors such as David Walliams, Enid Blyton, Astrid Lindgren and many more.

For a complete list of **Horrid Henry** titles visit

www.horridhenry.co.uk

or

www.orionchildrensbooks.co.uk

HORRID HENRY'S Halloween Horrors

Francesca Simon

Illustrated by Tony Ross

Orion
Children's Books

ORION CHILDREN'S BOOKS
This collection first published in Great Britain in 2017
by Hodder and Stoughton
3 5 7 9 10 8 6 4 2

A CIP catalogue record for this book
is available from the British Library.

ISBN 978 1 5101 0122 7

Printed and bound in Great Britain by Clays Ltd, St Ives plc

The paper and board used in this book are from
well-managed forests and other responsible sources.

FSC www.fsc.org
MIX
Paper from responsible sources
FSC® C104740

Orion Children's Books
An imprint of
Hachette Children's Books
Part of Hodder and Stoughton
Carmelite House
50 Victoria Embankment
London EC4Y 0DZ

An Hachette UK Company
www.hachette.co.uk
www.hachettechildrens.co.uk
www.horridhenry.co.uk

CONTENTS

HORRID HENRY'S TRICKS AND TREATS

Halloween! Oh happy, happy day! Every year Horrid Henry could not believe it: an entire day devoted to stuffing your face with sweets and playing horrid tricks. Best of all, you were *supposed* to stuff your face and play horrid tricks. Whoopee!

Horrid Henry was armed and ready. He had loo roll. He had water pistols. He had shaving foam. Oh my, would he be playing tricks tonight. Anyone who didn't instantly hand over a fistful of sweets would get it with the foam. And woe betide any fool who gave him an apple. Horrid Henry knew how to treat rotten grown-ups like that.

His red and black devil costume lay ready on the bed, complete with evil mask, twinkling horns, trident, and whippy tail. He'd scare everyone wearing that.

'Heh heh heh,' said Horrid Henry, practising his evil laugh.

'Henry,' came a little voice outside his bedroom door, 'come and see my new costume.'

'No,' said Henry.

'Oh please, Henry,' said his younger brother, Perfect Peter.

'No,' said Henry. 'I'm busy.'

'You're just jealous because *my* costume is nicer than yours,' said Peter.

'Am not.'

'Are too.'

Come to think of it, what *was* Peter wearing? Last year he'd copied Henry's monster costume and ruined Henry's Halloween. What if he were copying Henry's devil costume? That would be just like that horrible little copycat.

'All right, you can come in for two seconds,' said Henry.

A big, pink bouncy bunny bounded into Henry's room. It had little white bunny ears. It had a little white bunny tail. It had pink polka dots everywhere else. Horrid Henry groaned. What a stupid costume. Thank goodness *he* wasn't wearing it.

'Isn't it great?' said Perfect Peter.

'No,' said Henry. 'It's horrible.'

'You're just saying that to be mean, Henry,' said Peter, bouncing up and down. 'I can't wait to go trick-or-treating in it tonight.'

Oh no. Horrid Henry felt as if he'd been punched in the stomach. Henry would be expected to go out trick or treating – with Peter! He, Henry, would have to walk around with a pink polka dot bunny. Everyone would see him. The shame of it! Rude Ralph would never stop teasing him. Moody Margaret would call him a bunny wunny. How could he play tricks on people with a pink polka dot bunny following him everywhere? He was ruined. His name would be a joke.

'You can't wear that,' said Henry desperately.

'Yes I can,' said Peter.

'I won't let you,' said Henry.

Perfect Peter looked at Henry. 'You're just jealous.'

Grrr! Horrid Henry was about to tear that stupid costume off Peter when, suddenly, he had an idea.

It was painful.

It was humiliating.

But anything was better than having Peter prancing about in pink polka dots.

'Tell you what,' said Henry, 'just because I'm so nice I'll let you borrow my monster costume. You've always wanted to wear it.'

'NO!' said Peter. 'I want to be a bunny.'

'But you're supposed to be scary for Halloween,' said Henry.

'I am scary,' said Peter. 'I'm going to bounce up to people and yell 'boo'.'

'I can make you really scary, Peter,' said Horrid Henry.

'How?' said Peter.

'Sit down and I'll show you.' Henry patted his desk chair.

'What are you going to do?' said Peter suspiciously. He took a step back.

'Nothing,' said Henry. 'I'm just trying to help you.'

Perfect Peter didn't move.

'How can I be scarier?' he said cautiously.

'I can give you a scary haircut,' said Henry.

Perfect Peter clutched his curls.

'But I like my hair,' he said feebly.

'This is Halloween,' said Henry. 'Do you want to be scary or don't you?'

'Um, um, uh,' said Peter, as Henry pushed him down in the chair and got out the scissors.

'Not too much,' squealed Peter.

'Of course not,' said Horrid Henry. 'Just sit back and relax, I promise you'll love this.'

Horrid Henry twirled the scissors.

Snip! Snip! Snip! Snip! Snip!

★

Magnificent, thought Horrid Henry. He gazed proudly at his work. Maybe he should be a hairdresser when he grew up. Yes! Henry could see it now. Customers would queue for miles for one of

Monsieur Henri's scary snips. Shame his genius was wasted on someone as yucky as Peter. Still…

'You look great, Peter,' said Henry. 'Really scary. Atomic Bunny. Go and have a look.'

Peter went over and looked in the mirror.

'AAAAAAAAAARGGGGGG!'

'Scared yourself, did you?' said Henry. 'That's great.'

'AAAAAAAAAARGGGGGGG!' howled Peter.

Mum ran into the room.

'AAAAAAAAAARGGGGGG!' howled Mum.

'AAAAAAAAAARGGGGGGG!' howled Peter.

'Henry!' screeched Mum. 'What have you done! You horrid, horrid boy!'

What was left of Peter's hair stuck up in ragged tufts all over his head. On one side

was a big bald patch.
'I was just making him look scary,' protested Henry. 'He said I could.'

'Henry made me!' said Peter.

'My poor baby,' said Mum. She glared at Henry. 'No trick-or-treating for you,' said Mum. 'You'll stay here.'

Horrid Henry could hardly believe his ears. This was the worst thing that had ever happened to him.

'NO!' howled Henry. This was all Peter's fault.

'I hate you Peter!' he screeched. Then he attacked. He was Medusa, coiling round her victim with her snaky hair.

'Aaaahh!' screeched Peter.

'Henry!' shouted Mum. 'Go to your room!'

★

Mum and Peter left the house to go trick-or-treating. Henry had screamed and sobbed and begged. He'd put on his devil costume, just in case his tears melted their stony hearts. But no. His mean, horrible parents wouldn't change their mind. Well, they'd be sorry. They'd all be sorry.

Dad came into the sitting room. He was holding a large shopping bag.

'Henry, I've got some work to finish so I'm going to let you hand out treats to any trick-or-treaters.'

Horrid Henry stopped plotting his revenge. Had Dad gone mad? Hand out treats? What kind of punishment was this?

Horrid Henry fought to keep a big smile off his face.

'Here's the Halloween stuff, Henry,' said Dad. He handed Henry the heavy bag. 'But remember,' he added sternly, 'these treats are not for you: they're to give away.'

Yeah, right, thought Henry.

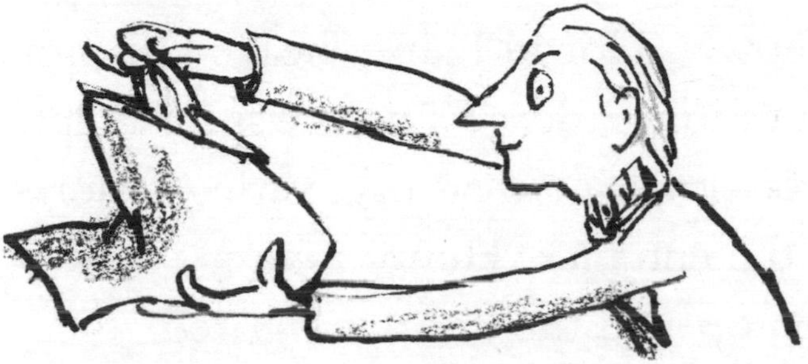

'OK Dad,' he said as meekly as he could. 'Whatever you say.'

Dad went back to the kitchen. Now was his chance! Horrid Henry leapt on the bag. Wow, was it full! He'd grab all the good stuff, throw back anything yucky with lime or peppermint, and he'd have enough sweets to keep him going for at least a week!

Henry yanked open the bag. A terrible sight met his eyes. The bag was full of satsumas. And apples. And walnuts in their shells. No wonder his horrible parents had trusted him to be in charge of it.

Ding dong.

Slowly, Horrid Henry heaved his heavy bones to the door. There was his empty, useless trick-or-treat bag, sitting forlornly by the entrance. Henry gave it a kick, then opened the door and glared.

'Whaddya want?' snapped Horrid Henry.

'Trick-or-treat,' whispered Weepy William. He was dressed as a pirate.

Horrid Henry held out the bag of horrors.

'Lucky dip!' he announced. 'Close your eyes for a big surprise!'

William certainly would be surprised at what a rotten treat he'd be getting.

Weepy William put down his swag bag, closed his eyes tight, then plunged his hand into Henry's lucky dip. He rummaged and he rummaged and he rummaged, hoping to find something better than satsumas.

Horrid Henry eyed Weepy William's bulging swag bag.

Go on Henry, urged the bag. He'll never notice.

Horrid Henry did not wait to be asked twice.

Dip!

Zip!

Pop!

Horrid Henry grabbed a big handful of William's sweets and popped them inside his empty bag.

Weepy William opened his eyes.

'Did you take some of my sweets?'

'No,' said Henry.

William peeked inside his bag and burst into tears.

'Waaaaaaaa!' wailed William. 'Henry took – '

Henry pushed him out and slammed the door.

Dad came running.

'What's wrong?'

'Nothing,' said Henry. 'Just William crying 'cause he's scared of pumpkins.'

Phew, thought Henry. That was close. Perhaps he had been a little too greedy.

Ding dong.

It was Lazy Linda wearing a pillowcase over her head. Gorgeous Gurinder was with her, dressed as a scarecrow.

'Trick-or-treat!'

'Trick-or-treat!'

'Close your eyes for a big surprise!' said Henry, holding out the lucky dip bag.

'Ooh, a lucky dip!' squealed Linda.

Lazy Linda and Gorgeous Gurinder put down their bags, closed their eyes, and reached into the lucky dip.

Dip!

Zip!

Pop!

Dip!

Zip!

Pop!

Lazy Linda opened her eyes.

'You give the worst treats ever, Henry,' said Linda, gazing at her walnut in disgust.

'We won't be coming back *here*,' sniffed Gorgeous Gurinder.

Tee hee, thought Horrid Henry.

Ding dong.

It was Beefy Bert. He was wearing a robot costume.

'Hi Bert, got any good sweets?' asked Henry.

'I dunno,' said Beefy Bert.

Horrid Henry soon found out that he did. Lots and lots and lots of them. So did Moody Margaret, Sour Susan, Jolly Josh and Tidy Ted. Soon Henry's bag was stuffed with treats.

Ding dong.

Horrid Henry opened the door.

'Boo,' said Atomic Bunny.

Henry's sweet bag! Help! Mum would see it!

'Eeeeek!' screeched Horrid Henry. 'Help! Save me!'

Quickly, he ran upstairs clutching his bag and hid it safely under his bed. Phew, that was close.

'Don't be scared, Henry, it's only me,' called Perfect Peter.

Horrid Henry came back downstairs.

'No!' said Henry. 'I'd never have known.'

'Really?' said Peter.

'Really,' said Henry.

'Everyone just gave sweets this year,' said Perfect Peter. 'Yuck.'

Horrid Henry held out the lucky dip.

'Ooh, a satsuma,' said Peter. 'Aren't I lucky!'

'I hope you've learned your lesson, Henry,' said Mum sternly.

'I certainly have,' said Horrid Henry, eyeing Perfect Peter's bulging bag. 'Good things come to those who wait.'

Henry's Halloween Howlers

Knock, knock.
Who's there?
Ivan.
Ivan who?
Ivan to suck your blood!

What do birds say
at Halloween?
Trick or tweet!

What's the best birthday
present for a skeleton?
A mobile bone.

How do you greet a three-headed monster?
Hello, hello, hello!

HORRID HENRY'S HAUNTED HOUSE

'No way!' shrieked Horrid Henry. He was not staying the weekend with his slimy cousin Stuck-up Steve, and that was that. He sat in the back seat of the car with his arms folded.

'Yes you are,' said Mum.

'Steve can't wait to see you,' said Dad.

This was not exactly true. After Henry had sprayed Steve with green goo last Christmas, *and* helped himself to a few of Steve's presents, Steve had sworn revenge. Under the circumstances,

Henry thought it would be a good idea to keep out of Steve's way.

And now Mum had arranged for him to spend the weekend while she and Dad went off on their own! Perfect Peter was staying with Tidy Ted, and he was stuck with Steve.

'It's a great chance for you boys to become good friends,' she said. 'Steve is a very nice boy.'

'I feel sick,' said Henry, coughing.

'Stop faking,' said Mum. 'You were well enough to play football all morning.'

'I'm too tired,' said Henry, yawning.

'I'm sure you'll get plenty of rest at Aunt Ruby's,' said Dad firmly.

'I'M NOT GOING!' howled Henry.

Mum and Dad took Henry by the arms, dragged him to Rich Aunt Ruby's door, and rang the bell.

The massive door opened immediately.

'Welcome, Henry,' said Rich Aunt Ruby, giving him a great smacking kiss.

'Henry, how lovely to see you,' said Stuck-up Steve sweetly. 'That's a very nice second-hand jumper you're wearing.'

'Hush, Steve,' said Rich Aunt Ruby. 'I think Henry looks very smart.'

Henry glared at Steve. Thank goodness he'd remembered his Goo-Shooter. He had a feeling he might need it.

'Goodbye, Henry,' said Mum. 'Be good. Ruby, thank you so much for having him.'

'Our pleasure,' lied Aunt Ruby.

The great door closed.

Henry was alone in the house with his arch-enemy.

Henry looked grimly at Steve. What a horrible boy, he thought.

Steve looked grimly at Henry. What a horrible boy, he thought.

'Why don't you both go upstairs and play in Steve's room till supper's ready?' said Aunt Ruby.

'I'll show Henry where he's sleeping first,' said Steve.

'Good idea,' said Aunt Ruby.

Reluctantly, Henry followed his cousin up the wide staircase.

'I bet you're scared of the dark,' said Steve.

''Course I'm not,' said Henry.

'That's good,' said Steve. 'This is my room,' he added, opening the door to an enormous bedroom. Horrid Henry stared longingly at the shelves filled to bursting with zillions of toys and games.

'Of course all *my* toys are brand new. Don't you dare touch anything,' hissed Steve. 'They're all mine and only *I* can play with them.'

Henry scowled. When he was king he'd use Steve's head for target practice.

They continued all the way to the top. Goodness, this old house was big, thought Henry.

Steve opened the door to a large attic bedroom, with brand new pink and blue flowered wallpaper, a four-poster bed, an enormous polished wood wardrobe, and two large windows.

'You're in the haunted room,' said Steve casually.

'Great!' said Henry. 'I love ghosts.' It would take more than a silly ghost to frighten *him*.

'Don't believe me if you don't want to,' said Steve. 'Just don't blame me when the ghost starts wailing.'

'You're nothing but a big fat liar,' said Henry. He was sure Steve was lying. He was absolutely sure Steve was lying. He was one million percent sure that Steve was lying.

He's just trying to pay me back for Christmas, thought Henry.

Steve shrugged. 'Suit yourself. See that stain on the carpet?'

Henry looked down at something brownish.

'That's where the ghost vaporized,' whispered Steve. 'Of course if you're too scared to sleep here . . .'

Henry would rather have walked on hot coals than admit being scared to Steve.

He yawned, as if he'd never heard anything so boring.

'I'm looking forward to meeting the ghost,' said Henry.

'Good,' said Steve.

'Supper, boys!' called Aunt Ruby.

Henry lay in bed. Somehow he'd survived the dreadful meal and Stuck-up Steve's bragging about his expensive clothes, toys and trainers. Now here he was, alone in the attic at the top of the house. He'd jumped into bed, carefully avoiding the faded brown patch on the floor. He was sure it was just spilled cola or something, but just in case …

Henry looked around him. The only thing he didn't like was the huge wardrobe opposite the bed. It loomed up in the darkness at him. You could hide a body in that wardrobe, thought Henry, then rather wished he hadn't.

'Ooooooooh.'

Henry stiffened.

Had he just imagined the sound of someone moaning?

Silence.

Nothing, thought Henry, snuggling down under the covers. Just the wind.

'Ooooooooh.'

This time the moaning was a fraction louder. The hairs on Henry's neck stood up. He gripped the sheets tightly.

'Haaaaaahhhhhh.'

Henry sat up.

'Haaaaaaaaahhhhhhhhhhh.'

The ghostly breathy moaning sound was not coming from outside. It appeared to be coming from inside the giant wardrobe.

Quickly, Henry switched on the bedside light.

What am I going to do? thought Henry. He wanted to run screaming to his aunt.

But the truth was, Henry was too frightened to move.

Some dreadful moaning thing was inside the wardrobe.

Just waiting to get *him*.

And then Horrid Henry remembered who he was. Leader of a pirate gang. Afraid of nothing (except injections).

I'll just get up and check inside that wardrobe, he thought. Am I a man or a mouse?

Mouse! he thought.

He did not move.

'Oooooooooaaaaahhhhhh,' moaned the THING. The unearthly noises were getting louder.

Shall I wait here for IT to get me, or shall I make a move first? thought Henry. Silently, he reached under the bed for his Goo-Shooter.

Then slowly, he swung his feet over the bed.

Tiptoe.

Tiptoe.

Tiptoe

Holding his breath, Horrid Henry stood outside the wardrobe.

'HAHAHAHAHAHAHAHAHHA!'

Henry jumped. Then he flung open the door and fired.

SPLAT!

'HAHAHAHAHAHAHAHAHAHAH AHAHAughhhhhhh –'

The wardrobe was empty.

Except for something small and greeny-black on the top shelf.

It looked like – it was!

Henry reached up and took it.

It was a cassette player. Covered in green goo.

Inside was a tape. It was called 'Dr Jekyll's Spooky Sounds.'

Steve, thought Horrid Henry grimly. REVENGE!

★

'Did you sleep well, dear?' asked Aunt Ruby at breakfast.

'Like a log,' said Henry.

'No strange noises?' asked Steve.

'No,' smiled Henry sweetly. 'Why, did you hear something?'

Steve looked disappointed. Horrid Henry kept his face blank. He couldn't wait for the evening.

★

Horrid Henry spent a busy day.
He went ice-skating.
He went to the cinema.
He played football.

After supper, Henry went straight to bed.

'It's been a lovely day,' he said. 'But I'm tired. Goodnight, Aunt Ruby. Goodnight, Steve.'

'Goodnight, Henry,' said Ruby.

Steve ignored him.

But Henry did not go to his bedroom. Instead he sneaked into Steve's.

He wriggled under Steve's bed and lay there, waiting.

Soon Steve came into the room. Henry resisted the urge to reach out and seize Steve's skinny leg. He had something much scarier in mind.

He heard Steve putting on his blue bunny pyjamas and jumping into bed. Henry waited until the room was dark.

Steve lay above him, humming to himself.

'Dooby dooby dooby do,' sang Steve.

Slowly, Henry reached up, and ever so slightly, poked the mattress.

Silence.

'Dooby dooby dooby do,' sang Steve, a little more quietly.

Henry reached up and poked the mattress again.

Steve sat up.

Then he lay back.

Henry poked the mattress again, ever so slightly.

'Must be my imagination,' muttered Steve.

Henry allowed several moments to pass. Then he twitched the duvet.

'Mummy,' whimpered Steve.

Jab! Henry gave the mattress a definite poke.

'AHHHHHHHHHHHH!' screamed Steve. He leaped up and ran out of the room. 'MUMMY! HELP! MONSTERS!'

Henry scrambled out of the room and ran silently up to his attic. Quick as he could he put on his pyjamas, then clattered noisily back down the stairs to Steve's.

Aunt Ruby was on her hands and knees, peering under the bed. Steve was shivering and quivering in the corner.

'There's nothing here, Steve,' she said firmly.

'What's wrong?' asked Henry.

'Nothing,' muttered Steve.

'You're not *scared* of the dark, are you?' said Henry.

'Back to bed, boys,' said Aunt Ruby. She left the room.

'Ahhhhh, Mummy, help! Monsters!' mimicked Henry, sticking out his tongue.

'MUM!' wailed Steve. 'Henry's being horrid!'

'GO TO BED, BOTH OF YOU!' shrieked Ruby.

'Watch out for monsters,' said Henry.

Steve did not move from his corner.

'Want to swap rooms tonight?' said Henry.

Steve did not wait to be asked twice.

'Oh yes,' said Steve.

'Go on up,' said Henry. 'Sweet dreams.'

Steve dashed out of his bedroom as fast as he could.

Tee hee, thought Horrid Henry, pulling Steve's toys down from the shelves. Now, what would he play with first?

Oh, yes. He'd left a few spooky sounds of his own under the attic bed – just in case.

Henry's Halloween Howlers

What is an ogre's favourite flavor squash?
Lemon and slime.

Why can't ghosts tell fibs?
Because you can see right through them.

Why do witches all look the same?
So you can't tell which witch is which.

Horrid Henry went to a Halloween party with a sheet on his head.
'Are you a ghost?' asked Rude Ralph.
'No, I'm an unmade bed.'

BURP!

HORRID HENRY WAKES THE DEAD

'No, no, no, no, no!' shouted Miss Battle-Axe. 'Spitting is not a talent, Graham. Violet, you can't do the can-can as your talent. Ralph, burping to the beat is not a talent.'

She turned to Bert. 'What's your talent?'

'I dunno,' said Beefy Bert.

'And what about you, Steven?' said Miss Battle-Axe grimly.

'Caveman,' grunted Stone-Age Steven. 'Ugg!'

Horrid Henry had had enough.

'Me next!' shrieked Horrid Henry. 'I've got a great talent! Me next!'

'Me!' shrieked Moody Margaret.

'Me!' shrieked Rude Ralph.

'No one who shouts out will be performing *anything*,' said Miss Battle-Axe.

Next week was Horrid Henry's school talent show. But this wasn't an ordinary school talent show. Oh no. This year was different. This year, the famous TV presenter Sneering Simone was choosing the winner.

But best and most fantastic of all, the prize was a chance to appear on Simone's TV programme *Talent Tigers*. And from there . . . well, there was no end to the fame and fortune which awaited the winner.

Horrid Henry had to win. He just had to. A chance to be on TV! A chance for his genius to be recognised, at last.

The only problem was, he had so many talents it was impossible to pick just one. He could eat crisps faster than Greedy Graham. He could burp to the theme tune of *Marvin the Maniac*. He could stick out his tongue almost as far as Moody Margaret.

But brilliant as these talents were, perhaps they weren't quite special enough to win. Hmmmm . . .

Wait, he had it.

He could perform his new rap, 'I have an ugly brother, ick ick ick/A smelly toad brother, who makes me sick.' That would be sure to get him on *Talent Tigers*.

'Margaret!' barked Miss Battle-Axe, 'what's your talent?'

'Susan and I are doing a rap,' said Moody Margaret.

What?

'*I'm* doing a rap,' howled Henry. How dare Margaret steal his idea!

'Only one person can do a rap,' said Miss Battle-Axe firmly.

'Unfair!' shrieked Horrid Henry.

'Be quiet, Henry,' said Miss Battle-Axe.

Moody Margaret stuck out her tongue at Horrid Henry. 'Nah nah ne nah nah.'

Horrid Henry stuck out his tongue at Moody Margaret. Aaaarrgh! It was so unfair.

'I'm doing a hundred push-ups,' said Aerobic Al.

'I'm playing the drums,' said Jazzy Jim.

'I want to do a rap!' howled Horrid Henry. 'Mine's much better than hers!'

'You have to do something else or not take part,' said Miss Battle-Axe, consulting her list.

Not take part? Was Miss Battle-Axe out of her mind? Had all those years working on a chain gang done her in?

Miss Battle-Axe stood in front of Henry, baring her fangs. Her pen tapped impatiently on her notebook.

'Last chance, Henry. List closes in ten seconds . . .'

What to do, what to do?

'I'll do magic,' said Horrid Henry. How hard could it be to do some magic? He wasn't a master of disguise and the fearless leader of the Purple Hand Gang for nothing. In fact, not only would he do magic, he would do the greatest magic trick the world had ever seen. No rabbits out of a hat. No flowers out of a cane. No sawing a girl in half – though if Margaret volunteered Henry would be very happy to oblige.

No! He, Henry, Il Stupendioso, the greatest magician ever, would . . . would . . . he would wake the dead.

Wow. That was much cooler than a rap. He could see it now. He would chant his magic spells and wave his magic wand, until slowly, slowly, slowly, out of the coffin the bony body would rise, sending the audience screaming out of the hall!

Yes! thought Horrid Henry, *Talent Tigers* here I come. All he needed was an assistant.

★

Unfortunately, no one in his class wanted to assist him.

'Are you crazy?' said Gorgeous Gurinder.

'I've got a much better talent than *that*. No way,' said Clever Clare.

'Wake the dead?' gasped Weepy William. 'Nooooo.'

Rats, thought Horrid Henry. For his spectacular trick to work, an assistant was essential. Henry hated working with other children, but sometimes it couldn't be helped. Was there anyone he knew who would do exactly as they were told? Someone who would obey his every order? Hmmm. Perhaps there was a certain someone who would even pay for the privilege of being in his show.

Perfect Peter was busy emptying the dishwasher without being asked.

'Peter,' said Henry sweetly, 'how much would you pay me if I let you be in my magic show?'

Perfect Peter couldn't believe his ears. Henry was asking him to be in his show. Peter had always wanted to be in a show. And now Henry was actually asking him after he'd said no a million times. It was a dream come true. He'd pay anything.

'I've got £6.27 in my piggy bank,' said Peter eagerly.

Horrid Henry pretended to think.

'Done!' said Horrid Henry. 'You can start by painting the coffin black.'

'Thank you, Henry,' said Peter humbly, handing over the money.

Tee hee, thought Horrid Henry, pocketing the loot.

Henry told Peter what he had to do. Peter's jaw dropped.

'And will my name be on the billboard so everyone will know I'm your assistant?' asked Peter.

'Of course,' said Horrid Henry.

★

The great day arrived at last. Henry had practised and practised and practised. His magic robes were ready. His magic spells were ready. His coffin was ready. His props were ready. Even his dead body was as ready as it would ever be. Victory was his!

Henry and Peter stood backstage and peeked through the curtain as the audience charged into the hall. The school was buzzing. Parents pushed and shoved to get the best seats. There was a stir as Sneering Simone swept in, taking her seat in the front row.

'Would you *please* move?' demanded Margaret's mother, waving her camcorder.

'I can't see my little Maggie Muffin.'

'And I can't see Al with your big head in the way,' snapped Aerobic Al's dad, shoving his camera in front of Moody Margaret's mum.

'Parents, behave!' shouted Mrs Oddbod. 'What an exciting programme we have for you today! You will be amazed at all the talents in this school. First Clare will recite pi, which as you all know is the ratio of the circumference of a circle to the diameter, to 31 significant figures!'

'3.14159 26535 89793 23846 26433 83279,' said Clever Clare.

Sneering Simone made a few notes.

'Boring,' shouted Horrid Henry. 'Boring!'

'Shhh,' hissed Miss Battle-Axe.

'Now, Gurinder, Linda, Fiona and Zoe proudly present: the cushion dance!'

Gorgeous Gurinder, Lazy Linda, Fiery Fiona and Zippy Zoe ran on stage and placed a cushion in each corner. Then they skipped to each pillow, pretended to sew it, then hopped around with a pillow each, singing:

'We're the stitching queens
dressed in sateen,
we're full of beans,
see us preen,
as we steal . . . the . . . scene!'

Sneering Simone looked surprised. Tee hee, thought Horrid Henry gleefully. If everyone's talents were as awful as that, he was a shoe-in for *Talent Tigers*.

'Lovely,' said Mrs Oddbod. 'Just lovely. And now we have William, who will play the flute.'

Weepy William put his mouth to the flute and blew. There was no sound. William stopped and stared at his flute. The mouth hole appeared to have vanished.

Everyone was looking at him. What could he do?

'Toot toot toot,' trilled William, pretending to blow. 'Toot toot toot-waaaaaah!' wailed William, bursting into tears and running off stage.

'Never mind,' said Mrs Oddbod, 'anyone could put the mouthpiece on upside down. And now we have . . .' Mrs Oddbod glanced at her paper, 'a caveman Ugga Ugg dance.'

Stone-Age Steven and Beefy Bert stomped on stage wearing leopard-skin costumes and carrying clubs.

'UGGG!' grunted Stone-Age Steven. 'UGGG UGGG UGGG UGGG UGGG! Me cave man!'

STOMP CLUMPA CLUMP
STOMP CLUMPA CLUMP
stomped Stone-Age Steven.

STOMP CLUMPA CLUMP
STOMP CLUMPA CLUMP
stomped Beefy Bert.

'UGGA BUG UGGA BUG UGG UGG UGG,' bellowed Steven, whacking the floor with his club.

'Bert!' hissed Miss Battle-Axe. 'This isn't your talent! What are you doing on stage?'

'I dunno,' said Beefy Bert.

'Boo! Boooooo!' jeered Horrid Henry from backstage as the Cavemen thudded off.

Then Moody Margaret and Sour Susan performed their rap:

'Mar-garet, ooh ooh oooh
Mar-garet, it's all true
Mar-garet, best of the best
Pick Margaret, and dump the rest'

Rats, thought Horrid Henry, glaring. My rap was so much better. What a waste. And why was the audience applauding?

'Booooo!' yelled Horrid Henry. 'Boooooo!'

'Another sound out of you and you will not be performing,' snapped Miss Battle-Axe.

'And now Soraya will be singing 'You broke my heart in 39 pieces', accompanied by her mother on the piano,' said Mrs Oddbod hastily.

'Sing out, Soraya!' hissed her mother, pounding the piano and singing along.

'I'm singing as loud as I can,' yelled Soraya.

BANG! BANG! BANG! BANG! BANG! BANG! went the piano.

Then Jolly Josh began to saw 'Twinkle twinkle little star' on his double bass.

Sneering Simone held her ears.

'We're next,' said Horrid Henry, grabbing hold of his billboard and whipping off the cloth.

Perfect Peter stared at the billboard. It read:

Il Stupendioso, world's greatest magician played by Henry

Magic by Henry
Costumes by Henry
Props by Henry
Sound by Henry
Written by Henry
Directed by Henry

'But Henry,' said Peter, 'where's my name?'

'Right here,' said Horrid Henry, pointing.

On the back, in tiny letters, was written:

Assistant: Peter

'But no one will see that,' said Peter.

Henry snorted.

'If I put your name on the *front* of the billboard, everyone would guess the trick,' said Henry.

'No they wouldn't,' said Peter.

Honestly, thought Horrid Henry, did

any magician ever have such a dreadful helper?

'I'm the star,' said Henry. 'You're lucky you're even in my show. Now shut up and get in the coffin.'

Perfect Peter was furious. That was just like Henry, to be so mean.

'Get in!' ordered Henry.

Peter put on his skeleton mask and climbed into the coffin. He was fuming.

Henry had said he'd put his name on the billboard, and then he'd written it on the back. No one would know he was the assistant. No one.

The lights dimmed. Spooky music began to play.

'Oooooooohhhh,' moaned the ghostly sounds as Horrid Henry, wearing his special long black robes studded with stars and a special magician's hat, dragged his coffin through the curtains onto the stage.

'I am Il Stupendioso, the great and powerful magician!' intoned Henry. 'Now, Il Stupendioso will perform the greatest trick ever seen. Be prepared to marvel. Be prepared to be amazed. Be prepared not to believe your eyes. I, Il Stupendioso, will wake the dead!!'

'Ooohh,' gasped the audience.

Horrid Henry swept back and forth across the stage, waving his wand and mumbling.

'First I will say the secret words of magic. Beware! Beware! Do not try this at home. Do not try this in a graveyard. Do not –' Henry's voice sank to a whisper – 'do not try this unless you're prepared for the dead . . . to walk!' Horrid Henry ended his sentence with a blood-curdling scream. The audience gasped.

Horrid Henry stood above the coffin and chanted:

'Abracadabra,
flummery flax,
voodoo hoodoo
mumbo crax.
Rise and shine, corpse of mine!'

Then Horrid Henry whacked the coffin once with his wand.

Slowly Perfect Peter poked a skeleton hand out of the coffin, then withdrew it.

'Ohhhh,' went the audience. Toddler Tom began to wail.

Horrid Henry repeated the spell.

'Abracadabra,
flummery flax,
voodoo hoodoo
mumbo crax.
Rise and shine, bony swine!'

Then Horrid Henry whacked the coffin twice with his wand.

This time Perfect Peter slowly raised the plastic skull with a few tufts of blond hair glued to it, then lowered it back down.

Toddler Tom began to howl.

'And now, for the third and final time, I will say the magic spell, and before your eyes, the body will rise. Stand back . . .

'Abracadabra,
flummery flax,
voodoo hoodoo
mumbo crax.
Rise and shine, here is the sign!'

And Horrid Henry whacked the coffin three times with his wand.

The audience held its breath.

And held it.

And held it.

And held it.

'He's been dead a long time, maybe his hearing isn't so good,' said Horrid Henry. 'Rise and shine, here is the sign,' shouted Henry, whacking the coffin furiously.

Again, nothing happened.

'Rise and shine, brother of mine,' hissed Henry, kicking the coffin, 'or you'll be sorry you were born.'

I'm on strike, thought Perfect Peter. How dare Henry stick his name on the back of the billboard. And after all Peter's hard work!

Horrid Henry looked at the audience. The audience looked expectantly at Horrid Henry.

What could he do? Open the coffin and yank the body out? Yell, 'Ta da!' and run off stage? Do his famous elephant dance?

Horrid Henry took a deep breath.

'Now that's what I call *dead*,' said Horrid Henry.

★

'This was a difficult decision,' said Sneering Simone. Henry held his breath. He'd kill Peter later. Peter had finally risen from the coffin *after* Henry left the stage, then instead of slinking off, he'd actually said, 'Hello everyone! I'm alive!' and waved. Grrr. Well, Peter wouldn't have to pretend to be a corpse once Henry had finished with him.

'. . . a very difficult decision. But I've decided that the winner is . . .' Please not Margaret, please not Margaret, prayed Henry. Sneering Simone consulted her notes, 'The winner is the Il Stupendioso–'

'YES!!' screamed Horrid Henry, leaping to his feet. He'd done it! Fame at last! Henry Superstar was born! Yes yes yes!

Sneering Simone glared. 'As I was saying, the Il Stupendioso corpse. Great comic timing. Can someone tell me his name?'

Horrid Henry stopped dancing.

Huh?

What?

The *corpse*?

'Is that me?' said Peter. '*I* won?'

'NOOOOOOOOO!' shrieked Horrid Henry.

Henry's Halloween Howlers

Why was the skeleton afraid of the dog?
Because dogs like bones!

What should you do after shaking hands with a monster?
Count your fingers.

What kind of music does a mummy listen to?
Wrap music.

What did the pirate get when he hit the skeleton?
A skull and very cross bones.

Zombie
Vampires

HORRID HENRY AND THE ZOMBIE VAMPIRE

'Isn't it exciting, Henry?' said Perfect Peter, packing Bunnykins carefully in his Sammy the Snail overnight bag. 'A museum sleepover! With a torch-lit trail! And worksheets! I can't think of anything more fun.'

'I can,' snarled Horrid Henry. Being trapped in a cave with Clever Clare reciting all the multiplication tables from one to a million. Watching *Cooking Cuties*. Even visiting Nurse Needle for one of her horrible injections. (Well, maybe not *that*).

But *almost* anything would be better than being stuck overnight in Our Town Museum on a class sleepover. No TV. No computers. No comics. Why oh why did he have to do this? He wanted to sleep in his own comfy bed, not in a sleeping bag on the museum's cold hard floor, surrounded by photos of old mayors and a few dusty exhibits.

AAARRRRRGGGHH. Wasn't it bad enough he was bored all day in school without being bored all night too?

Worse, Peter's nappy baby class was coming, too. They'd probably have to be tucked in at seven o'clock, when they'd all start crying for their mamas. Ugghh. And then Miss Battle-

Axe snarling at them to finish their worksheets, and Moody Margaret snoring and Anxious Andrew whimpering that he'd seen a ghost . . .

Well, no way was he going to that boring old dump without some comics to pass the time. He'd just bought the latest *Screamin' Demon* with a big article all about vampires and zombies. Yay! He couldn't wait to read it.

Perfect Peter watched him stuff his Mutant Max bag full of comics.

'Henry, you know we're not allowed to bring comics to the museum sleepover,' said Perfect Peter.

'Shut up and mind your own business, toad,' said Horrid Henry.

'Mum! Henry just called me a toad!' wailed Peter. 'And he told me to shut up.'

'Toady Toady Toady, Toady Toady Toady,' jeered Henry.

'Henry! Stop being horrid or no museum sleepover for you,' yelled Mum.

Horrid Henry paused. Was it too late to be horrid enough to get banned from the sleepover? Why hadn't he thought of this before? Why, he could . . .

'Henry! Peter! We have to leave *now*!' yelled Dad.

Rats.

★

The children queued up in the museum's Central Hall clutching their sleeping bags as Miss Lovely and Miss Battle-Axe ticked off names on a big register.

'Go away, Susan,' said Moody Margaret. 'After what you did at my house I'm going to sit with Gurinder. So there.'

'You're such a meanie, Margaret,' said Sour Susan.

'Am not.'

'Are too.'

Susan scowled. Margaret was *always* so mean. If only she could think of a way to pay that old grouch back.

Margaret scowled. Susan was *always* so annoying. If only she could think of a way to pay that old fraidy cat back.

Henry scowled. Why did he have to be here? What he'd give for a magic carpet to whisk him straight home to the comfy black chair to watch *Terminator Gladiator*. Could life get any worse?

'Henwy,' came a little voice next to him. 'I love you Henwy. I want to give you a big kiss.'

Oh no, thought Horrid Henry. Oh no. It was Lisping Lily, New Nick's little sister. What was that foul fiend doing here?

'You keep away from me,' said Horrid Henry, pushing and shoving his way through the children to escape her.

'Waaa!' wept Weepy William as Henry stepped on his foot.

'I want my mama,' cried Needy Neil as Henry trampled on his sleeping bag.

'But I want to marry with you, Henwy,' lisped Lily, trying to follow him.

'Henry! Stay still!' barked Miss Battle-Axe, glaring at him with her demon eyes.

'Hello boys and girls, what an adventure we're going to have tonight,' said the museum's guide, Earnest Ella, as she handed out pencils and worksheets.

Henry groaned. Boring! He hated worksheets.

'Did you know that our museum has a famous collection of balls of wool through the ages?' droned Earnest Ella. 'And an old railway car? Oh yes, it's going to be an exciting sleepover night. We're even going on a torch-lit walk through the corridors.'

Horrid Henry yawned and sneaked a peek at his comic book, which he'd hidden beneath his museum worksheet.

Watch out, Demon Fans!! To celebrate the release of this season's big blockbuster monster horror film, THE ZOMBIE VAMPIRES, study this check-list. Make sure there are no zombie-vampires lurking in your neighbourhood!!!!

Horrid Henry gasped as he read *How To Recognise a Vampire* and *How to Recognise a Zombie*. Big scary teeth?

Big googly eyes? Looks like the walking dead? Wow, that described Miss Battle-Axe perfectly. All they had to add was a big fat carrot nose and . . .

A dark shadow loomed over him.

'I'll take that,' snapped Miss Battle-Axe, yanking the comic out of his hand. '*And* the rest.'

Huh?

He'd been so careful. How had she spotted that comic under his worksheet?

And how did she know about the secret stash in his bag? Horrid Henry looked round the hall. Aha! There was Peter, pretending not to look at him. How dare that wormy worm toad tell on him? Just for that . . .

'Come along everyone, line up to collect your torches for our spooky walk,' said Earnest Ella. 'You wouldn't want to get left behind in the dark, would you?'

There was no time to lose. Horrid Henry slipped over to Peter's class and joined him in line with Tidy Ted and Goody Goody Gordon.

'Hello Peter,' said Henry sweetly.

Peter looked at him nervously. Did Henry suspect *he'd* told on him? Henry didn't *look* angry.

'Shame my comic got confiscated,' said Henry, ''cause it had a list of how to tell whether anyone you know is a zombie vampire.'

'A zombie vampire?' said Tidy Ted.

'Yup,' said Henry.

'They're imaginary,' said Goody-Goody Gordon.

'That's what they'd *like* you to believe,' said Henry. 'But I've discovered some.'

'Where?' said Ted.

Horrid Henry looked around dramatically, then dropped his voice to a whisper.

'Two teachers at our school,' hissed Henry.

'Two *teachers*?' said Peter.

'What?' said Ted.

'You heard me. Zombie vampires. Miss Battle-Axe *and* Miss Lovely.'

'Miss *Lovely*?' gasped Peter.

'You're just making that up,' said Gordon.

'It was all in *Screamin' Demon*,' said Henry. 'That's why Miss Battle-Axe snatched my comic. To stop me finding out the truth. Listen carefully.'

Henry recited:

'How to recognise a vampire:
1. BIG HUGE SCARY TEETH.'

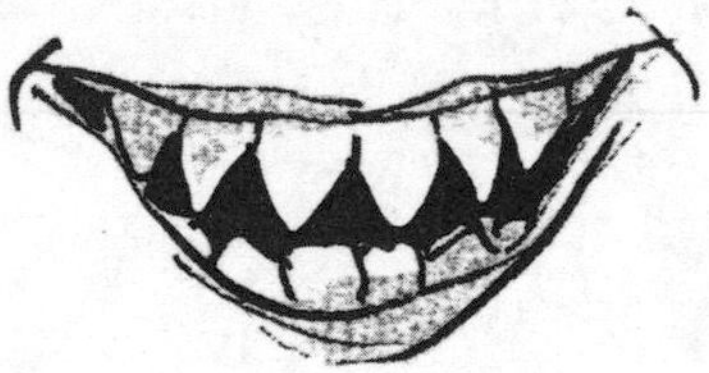

'If Miss Battle-Axe's fangs were any bigger she would trip over them,' said Horrid Henry.

Tidy Ted nodded. 'She *does* have big pointy teeth.'

'That doesn't prove anything,' said Peter.

'2. DRINKS BLOOD.'

Perfect Peter shook his head. 'Drinks . . . blood?'

'*Obviously* they do, just not *in front* of people,' said Horrid Henry. 'That would give away their terrible secret.'

'3. ONLY APPEARS AT NIGHT.'

'But Henry,' said Goody-Goody Gordon, 'we see Miss Battle-Axe and Miss Lovely every day at school. They *can't* be vampires.'

Henry sighed. 'Have you been paying attention? I didn't say they were *vampires*, I said they were *zombie* vampires. Being half-zombie lets them walk about in daylight.'

Perfect Peter and Goody-Goody Gordon looked at one another.

'Here's the total proof,' Henry continued.

'How to recognise a zombie:
1. LOOKS DEAD.'

'Does Miss Battle-Axe look dead? Definitely,' said Horrid Henry. 'I never saw a more dead-looking person.'

'But Henry,' said Peter. 'She's alive.'

Unfortunately, yes, thought Horrid Henry.

'Duh,' he said. 'Zombies always *seem* alive. Plus, zombies have got scary, bulging eyes like Miss Battle-Axe,' continued Henry. 'And they feed on human flesh.'

'Miss Lovely doesn't eat human flesh,' said Peter. 'She's a vegetarian.'

'A likely story,' said Henry.

'You're just trying to scare us,' said Peter.

'Don't you see?' said Henry. 'They're planning to pounce on us during the torch-lit trail.'

'I don't believe you,' said Peter.

Henry shrugged. 'Fine. Don't believe me. Just don't say I didn't warn you when Miss Lovely lurches out of the dark and BITES you!' he shrieked.

'Be quiet, Henry,' shouted Miss Battle-Axe. 'William. Stop weeping.

There's nothing to be scared of. Linda! Stand up. It's not bedtime yet. Bert! Where's your torch?'

'I dunno,' said Beefy Bert.

Miss Lovely walked over and smiled at Peter.

'Looking forward to the torchlit walk?' she beamed.

Peter couldn't stop himself sneaking a peek at her teeth. *Were* they big? And sharp? Funny, he'd never noticed before how pointy two of them were . . . And was her face a bit . . . umm . . . pale?

No! Henry was just trying to trick him. Well, he wasn't going to be fooled.

'Time to go exploring,' said Earnest Ella. 'First stop on the torch-lit trail: our brand-new exhibit, *Wonderful World of Wool*. Then we'll be popping next door down the *Passage to the Past* to visit the old railway car and the Victorian shop

and a Neanderthal cave. Torches on, everyone.'

★

Sour Susan smiled to herself. She'd just thought of the perfect revenge on Margaret for teasing her for being such a scaredy cat.

Moody Margaret smiled to herself. She'd just thought of the perfect revenge on Susan for being so sour.

Ha ha Margaret, thought Susan. I'll get you tonight.

Ha ha Susan, thought Margaret. I'll get you tonight.

Ha ha Peter, thought Henry. I'll get you tonight.

★

'Follow me,' said Earnest Ella.

The children stampeded after her.

All except three.

When the coast was clear, Moody Margaret turned off her torch, darted into the pitch-black *Passage to the Past* hall and hid in the Neanderthal cave behind the caveman. She'd leap out at Susan when she walked past. MWAHAHAHAHAHAHA! Wouldn't that old scaredy cat get a fright.

Sour Susan turned off her torch and peeked down the *Passage to the Past* corridor. Empty. She tiptoed to the railway car and crept inside. Just wait till Margaret walked by . . .

Horrid Henry turned off his torch, crept down the *Passage to the Past*, sneaked into the Victorian shop and hid behind the rocking chair.

Tee hee. Just wait till Peter walked past. He'd—

What was that?

Was it his imagination? Or did that spinning wheel in the corner of the shop . . . move?

CR—EEEK went the wheel.

It was so dark. But Henry didn't dare switch on his torch.

Moody Margaret looked over from the Neanderthal cave at the Victorian shop. Was it her imagination or was that rocking chair rocking back and forth?

Sour Susan looked out from the railway car. Was it her imagination or was the caveman moving? There was a strange, scuttling noise. What was that? thought Susan.

You know, thought Henry, this museum *is* kind of creepy at night.

And then something grabbed onto his leg.

'AAAARRRRGGHHH!' screamed Horrid Henry.

★

Moody Margaret heard a blood-curdling scream. Scarcely daring to breathe, Margaret peeped over the caveman's shoulder . . .

Sour Susan heard a blood-curdling scream. Scarcely daring to breathe, Susan peeped out from the railway carriage . . .

★

'Henwy, I found you, Henwy,' piped the creature clinging to his leg.

'Go away Lily,' hissed Henry. The horrible fiend was going to ruin everything.

'Will you marry me, Henwy?'

'No!' said Horrid Henry, trying to shake her off and brushing against the spinning wheel.

CR—EEEEK.

The spinning wheel spun.

What's that noise? thought Margaret, craning to see from behind the caveman.

'Henwy! I want to give you a big kiss,' lisped Lily.

Horrid Henry shook his leg harder.

The spinning wheel tottered and fell over.

CRASH!

Margaret and Susan saw something lurch out of the Victorian shop and loom up in the darkness. A monstrous creature with four legs and waving arms . . .

'AAAARRRRGGHH!' screamed Susan.

'AAAARGGHHHHH!' shrieked Margaret.

'AAAARGGHHHHH!' shrieked Henry.

★

The unearthly screams rang through the museum. Peter, Ted, and Gordon froze.

'You don't think—' gasped Gordon.

'Not . . . ' trembled Peter.

'Zombie vampires?' whimpered Ted. They clutched one another.

'Everyone head back to the Central Hall NOW!' shouted Earnest Ella.

★

In the cafeteria, Miss Lovely and Miss Battle-Axe were snatching a short break to enjoy a lovely fried egg sandwich with lashings of ketchup.

Oh my weary bones, thought Miss Battle-Axe, as she sank her teeth into the huge sandwich. Peace at last.

AAARRGGHH! EEEEEKKK! HELLLP!

Miss Battle-Axe and Miss Lovely squeezed their sandwiches in shock as they heard the terrible screams.

SPLAT!

A stream of ketchup squirted Miss Lovely in the eye and dripped down her face onto her blouse.

SQUIRT!

A blob of ketchup splatted Miss Battle-Axe on the nose and dribbled down her chin onto her cardigan.

'Sorry, Boudicca,' said Miss Lovely.

'Sorry, Lydia,' said Miss Battle-Axe.

They raced into the dark Central Hall just as their classes ran back from the torch-lit walk. Fifty beams of light from fifty torches lit up the teachers' ketchup-covered faces and ketchup-stained clothes.

'AAAARRGGHHH!' screamed Perfect Peter.

'It's the zombie vampires!' howled Tidy Ted.

'Run for your lives!' yelped Goody-Goody Gordon.

'Wait!' shouted Miss Lovely! 'Children, come back!'

'We won't eat you!' shouted Miss Battle-Axe.

'AAAARRRRGGHHHHHH!'

Henry's Halloween Howlers

How do you make
a witch itch?
Take away the W.

What goes 'Flap, flap! Bite, bite! Ouch, ouch!'
Dracula with toothache.

Who writes
invisible books?
Ghost writers.

What do ghosts
spread on bagels?
Scream cheese.

HORRID HENRY'S NIGHTMARE

'. . . and then the slime-covered, flesh-eating zombie, fangs dripping blood, lurched into school, wailing and gnashing and – **pouncing**!' screamed Rude Ralph, grabbing Horrid Henry.

Henry shrieked.

'Ha ha, gotcha,' said Ralph.

Horrid Henry's heart pounded. How he loved being scared! What could be better than having a sleepover with Ralph, and both of them trying to scare the other? He reached into the Purple

Hand Fort's top secret skull and bones biscuit tin, and scoffed a big handful of chocolate gooey chewies. Scary stories and chocolate. Whoopie!

'Watch out, Ralph,' said Henry. 'I'm gonna tell you about the alien acid monster who creeps— '

'Smelly toads,' piped a little voice outside the Purple Hand Fort.

Grrr.

'Hide,' hissed Horrid Henry.

Rude Ralph belched.

'I know you're in there, Henry,' said Peter.

'No I'm not,' said Henry.

'And I said the password, so you have to let me in,' said Peter. 'It's my fort too. Mum said so.'

Horrid Henry sighed loudly. Why on earth, of all the possible brothers in the world, did he have to get stuck with Peter? Why oh why, when younger brothers were being distributed, did he get landed with a tell-tale, smelly nappy baby?

'All right, come in,' said Henry.

Perfect Peter crept through the branches.

'Why is it so dark in here?' said Peter.

'None of your business, baby,' said Henry. 'You've been in, now get out.'

'Yeah, wriggle off, worm,' said Ralph.

'No babies allowed in the Purple Hand Fort,' said Henry.

Perfect Peter stuck out his lower lip.

'I'm going to tell Mum you wouldn't let me stay in the fort. And that you called me a baby.'

'Go ahead, baby boo boo,' said Henry.

'MUM!' screamed Peter. 'Henry called me baby boo boo.'

'Stop being horrid, Henry, and be nice to your brother,' shouted Mum. 'Or I'll send Ralph home.'

'I wasn't being horrid,' bellowed Henry. Oh to be a wizard and turn Peter into a toadstool.

'Okay, Peter, you can stay,' snarled Henry. 'But you'll be sorry.'

'No I won't,' said Peter.

'We're telling scary stories,' said Ralph.

'And you hate scary stories,' said Henry.

Peter considered. It was true, he hated being scared. And almost everything scared him. But maybe that was last week. Maybe now that he was a week older he wouldn't be scared any more.

'I'm brave now,' said Peter.

Horrid Henry shrugged. 'Well, just don't blame me when you wake up screaming tonight,' he shrieked.

Peter jumped. Should he stay and listen to these terrible tales? Then he squared his shoulders. He wasn't a baby, whatever Henry said. He was a big boy.

Horrid Henry told his scariest story about the child-eating vampire werewolf. Rude Ralph told his scariest story about the wailing graveyard ghost who slurped up babies. Then Henry told his most scary story ever in the history of the world: the alien acid monster and zombie mummy who—

'I know a scary story,' interrupted Peter.

'We don't want to hear it,' said Henry.

'It's really scary, I promise,' said Peter. 'Once upon a time there was a bunny . . .'

'SCARY stories!' shouted Rude Ralph.

'Once upon a time there was a really big bunny,' said Peter. 'And one day his little tail fell off.'

Peter paused.

'Is that it?' said Henry.

'Yes,' said Peter.

'Bleccccchhhh,' belched Rude Ralph.

'That's your idea of a scary story?' said Henry. 'A bunny with no tail?'

'Wouldn't you be scared if you were a bunny and your tail fell off?' said Peter.

'Isn't it time for you to practise your cello?' said Henry.

Peter gasped.

He didn't ever like to miss a day's practice.

Perfect Peter trotted off.

Phew. Worm-free at last.

'Now, as I was telling you, Ralph,' said Horrid Henry, 'there was once a zombie mummy that roamed . . .'

★

NO!!!!!

Horrid Henry lay in bed in his dark bedroom, trembling. What a horrible, horrible nightmare. All about a ghost bunny with huge teeth and no tail, charging at him waving a gigantic needle. Ugggh. His heart was pounding so fast he thought it would pop out of his chest.

But what to do, what to do?

Henry was too scared to stay in bed. Henry was too scared to move. Don't be an idiot, snarled Devil 1. There is no such thing as a ghost bunny. Yeah, you lummox, snarled Devil 2. What a wimp. Frankly, I'm disappointed.

But Horrid Henry was too terrified to

listen to reason. What if that alien acid monster or the ghost bunny was hiding under his bed? Horrid Henry wanted to lean over and check, but he couldn't.

Because what if the wailing graveyard ghost had sneaked into his wardrobe and was just waiting to GRAB him?

Worst of all, there was Ralph, snoring happily away in his sleeping bag. How could he just lie there when he was going to get gobbled up any second?

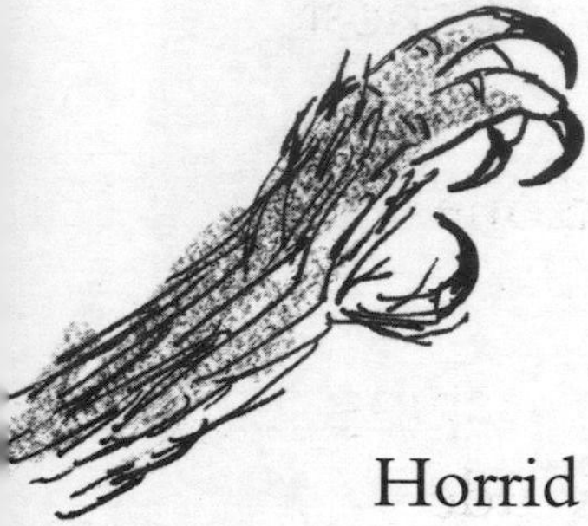

'Ralph,' hissed Henry.

'Shut up,' mumbled Ralph, rudely.

'I'm . . .' But what could Horrid Henry say? If he told Ralph he was – Horrid Henry could barely even think the word – scared, he'd never hear the end of it. Everyone would call him, Henry, leader of the Purple Hand Gang, a goochy goochy nappy baby.

Yikes.

Should he stay in bed and get eaten by the alien acid monster, or get out of bed and get eaten by the wailing graveyard ghost?

Actually, thought Horrid Henry, the acid monster would get Ralph first, since he was asleep on the floor. But if he jumped really fast, he could race out the door and down the hall to Mum and Dad's room before the graveyard ghost could grab him.

But should he leave Ralph alone to face the monsters?

Yes! thought Horrid Henry, leaping out of bed and trampling on Rude Ralph's head.

'Uhhh,' groaned Ralph. 'Watch where you're going, you big fat . . .'

But Horrid Henry wasn't listening. He stampeded to the bedroom door, dashed

into the dark hallway and slammed the door behind him. Right now he was so scared he didn't care if he was too old to jump into Mum and Dad's bed.

Phew. Horrid Henry paused, gasping for breath.

He was safe. The monsters would be too busy chomping on Ralph to nab him.

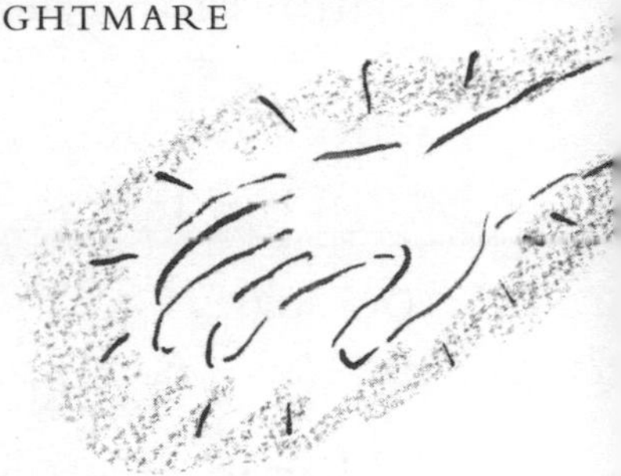

But wait. Could the graveyard ghost ooze under the door and grab him in the hall? Worse, was the injection bunny gliding up the stairs?

Horrid Henry froze. Oh no. His heart was pounding.

He opened his mouth to shriek 'MUM!'

Then he closed it.

Wait a minute. Wait a minute.

Peter was sure to be awake, after all the horrible scary stories he'd heard today. After all, Peter was the biggest scaredy-cat ever. If Henry was scared, Peter would be a dripping wreck.

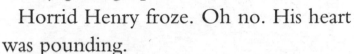

He'd just drop in. Seeing Peter terrified would make him feel a whole lot better, and a whole lot braver.

I'll bet Peter's lying there shaking and too scared to move, thought Horrid Henry. Ha. Ha. Ha.

Horrid Henry crept into Peter's room and shut the door. Then he tip-toed over to Peter's bed . . .

Huh?

There was Peter, sound asleep, a sweet smile on his face, his peaceful face lit up by his bunny nightlight and ceiling stars.

Horrid Henry's jaw dropped. How could Peter not be having horrible nightmares too? It was so unfair! He was the brave one, scared of nothing (except injections) and Peter was the wormy worm wibble pants noodle-head who was scared of Rudy the Rootin-Tootin Rooster cartoon, Santa Claus, and probably the Tooth Fairy.

Well, he'd do something about that.

'Slimy acid monster,' murmured Henry in Peter's ear. 'Coming to get you with his great big googly eyes and great big monster teeth. Be afraid, Peter. Be very afraid. OOOOOOOOOOOOOHHH.'

Perfect Peter smiled in his sleep.

'Hello Mr Monster,' he said.

'BOO!' said Horrid Henry. 'BOOO!'

'Would you like a cup of tea?' murmured Peter.

'No,' growled Horrid Henry. 'I want to eat YOU!'

'Okay,' said Peter drowsily.

What was wrong with him? thought Horrid Henry.

'**Mwaahahahahahaha**,' cackled Horrid Henry. '**I'm the graveyard ghost come to GET ya**.'

'That's nice,' murmured Peter.

'No, it's not nice,' growled Horrid Henry. 'It's scary. It's terrible. Woooooooooo! Arrrrggghhhhh!

BOOOOOO-OOOOO-OOO!'

Suddenly Peter's door opened.

'AAAAAAAARRRRGGGHHH!' screamed Horrid Henry.

'AAAAAAAARRRRGGGHHH!' screamed Perfect Peter.

'What are you doing in here, Henry?' said Mum.

'It's 3 o'clock in the morning,' said Dad.

Horrid Henry was never so happy to see anyone in his life.

'I thought Peter would be scared, so I came in to check on him,' said Horrid Henry.

Mum stared at Henry.

'And why did you think Peter would be scared?' asked Mum. She looked suspiciously at Henry.

''Cause I just did,' said Henry.

'Go back to your room, Henry,' said Mum.

His room? His haunted horrible room where all the monsters were lurking?

'Mum, could you just come with me?' said Henry. 'I need you to check on something.'

'Can't it wait till morning?' said Dad, yawning.

'No,' said Horrid Henry. 'I think there's a tarantula under my bed. Could you check please?'

After all, if Mum saw an acid alien there instead of a tarantula, she'd probably mention it.

Mum sighed, walked him to his room and checked under the bed.

'There's nothing there,' said Mum.

'Oh, and in my wardrobe, I'm sure I saw a . . . umm . . . mouse run in,' said Henry. 'That's what woke me. Could you just check for me?'

Mum looked in the wardrobe.

'That's it, Henry,' snapped Mum. 'Now go to sleep.'

Horrid Henry climbed back into bed and sighed happily. His room looked just as friendly and familiar as usual.

Why on earth had he been scared?

'Pssst, Ralph, you awake?' hissed Henry.

'Yeah,' said Rude Ralph, sitting up.

'Wanna hear a scary story?' said Henry. 'I know a great one about a mouldering monster and a cursed monkey paw . . .'

'Yeah!' said Rude Ralph.

Henry's Halloween Howlers

DRACULA'S SCHOOL REPORT

Reading: *better in the dark*

Writing: *upside down*

Cricket: *shows promise as a bat*

Who did Dracula fall in love with?

The girl necks door.

Why did the monster cross the road?

To eat the chicken.

Why was the
monster called Fog?
*Because he was thick
and grey.*

What does the polite monster say when
he meets people for the first time?
Pleased to eat you.

What did the monster
eat at Restaurant
Le Posh?
The waiter.

What instrument
do skeletons play?
Trombone.

HORRID HENRY'S CANNIBAL CURSE

It was the weekend. Yippee! No school. No school dinners. No Miss Battle-Axe. And best of all, no homework.

It was the weekend. Boo. Hiss. Yuck. The weekend meant . . . chores. His mean horrible parents weren't happy with torturing him by sending him to school five days a week and then making him live with wormy worm Peter the rest of the time.

Oh no. They had to make him suffer as their slave as well. Did they have any idea how much time doing chores took? How much wonderful telly he missed trudging up and down the stairs emptying all the waste paper baskets and cleaning out Fluffy's litter tray and putting the recycling outside?

Horrid Henry had lost hours. Months. Years of his life.

It was so unfair.

One day, one happy day, he would find a way to get out of this weekly misery. One day he would find a slave of his own who he could boss around.

Perfect Peter bounced into the sitting room and went to the bookshelf.

'Go away,' said Horrid Henry.

'What are you doing, Henry?' asked Peter. 'I'm going to alphabetise my books.'

'What does it look like I'm doing, Poopsicle?' said Henry, stretching out on the sofa. If only he didn't have to move.

'I'm not a poopsicle,' said Peter.

Horrid Henry looked at Peter the poopsicle. And then Horrid Henry had a brilliant, wonderful, spectacular idea. Why oh why hadn't he thought of this before?

'It's sad you're such a baby,' said Henry.

'I am not a baby,' said Peter. 'I'm a big boy. Mum said so.'

'Do you really think you're as good as me?' said Henry. 'That anything I can do you can do?'

'Yes,' said Peter.

Of course he was as good as Henry. Better, in fact, but Perfect Peter didn't want to brag. Peter was definitely smarter. And kinder. And tidier. And he had more money in his piggy bank. And he could play the cello.

In fact the only thing Henry could do better than him was run a teensy weensy bit faster.

'I can do anything you can do,' said Peter.

'No way, Uggalina,' said Henry.

'You're a baby.'

'Am not,' said Peter. 'And don't call me Uggalina.'

'Then I dare you to run upstairs and collect all the recycling,' said Horrid Henry. 'Bet you can't do it by the time I count to twenty-five.'

'Can too,' said Peter.

'Nah,' said Henry. 'You're much too little.'

'Am not,' said Peter.

'Then prove it, baby boo boo,' said Henry. 'If you can, you'll never be a baby boo boo again.'

Perfect Peter grabbed a rubbish bag and dashed upstairs.

Horrid Henry leaned back on the sofa and counted loudly.

Tee hee.

What a brilliant way to get Peter to do his chores.

Peter dashed downstairs, gasping for breath, clutching a full bag.

'Nineteen . . . twenty . . . Peter, you did it,' said Henry. 'You're king of the rubbish.'

Perfect Peter was delighted. It wasn't often that Henry praised him.

'I knew I could do it,' said Peter, trying to stop panting. He'd never run so fast in his life.

'Wow,' said Henry. 'You really proved me wrong.'

Peter glowed. Finally, finally, Henry was recognising how clever he was. And no more being called baby boo boo.

'That was amazing,' said Henry. 'Now, let's see how fast you can clean out Fluffy's litter tray. My best time is fifty-four seconds. I'll start counting . . . now. One. Two. Thr—'

Perfect Peter raced to Fluffy's stinky

litter box by the kitchen back door. He'd show Henry how fast he was. Henry would never be able to call him a nappy baby wibble pants again.

Peter grabbed the poop scoop.

Then he stopped.

A terrible thought dribbled into his brain.

Was it possible?

Was Henry tricking him? Tricking him into doing his chores? Had he fallen for Henry's tricks . . . again??

Perfect Peter smelled a rat.

No. No. NOOOOOOO!

'Mum,' wailed Peter. 'Henry tricked me into doing his chores.'

Uh oh, thought Henry.

'Don't be horrid, Henry,' shouted Mum. 'Do your own chores or no TV for a week.'

'I don't know what you're talking about,' bellowed Henry. 'We were just having a race.'

Perfect Peter came back into the room. He wanted to pour cat litter all over Henry, and kick the recycling bag.

'Do it,' said his devil. 'Live for once.'

'Don't do it,' said his angel. 'Then you'd be horrid too.'

Eeeeeek.

'Tell-tale,' hissed Henry.

'Serves you right, Henry,' said Peter. How could he have thought Henry was being nice to him for once? He swore he'd never fall for one of Henry's tricks ever ever again.

Peter glared at Henry.

Henry smiled at Peter.

'I've written a song for you, Peter,' said Horrid Henry.

He jumped on the sofa and began to sing:

'Oh I'm a big fat ninny
A skinny minny ninny
I'm a strudel-noodle tart
And all I do is far—'

'Mum,' screamed Peter. 'Henry called me a ninny. And a strudel-noodle.'

'Did not,' said Horrid Henry. 'I was just singing a song.'

'That's it, Henry,' said Mum, running into the room. 'No pocket money for a week.'

No pocket money? And all because of his wormy worm brother?

'But I wasn't doing anything,' howled Henry. 'Is it a crime to sing a song in this house?'

★

Ding Dong.

It was Rude Ralph come over to play. He was holding a lumpy plastic bag. They went up to Henry's bedroom.

'No worms allowed,' said Henry, slamming the door. He had to pay Peter back for getting him into trouble for singing. It was so unfair.

'What's in the bag?' said Horrid Henry.

'Shrunken heads,' said Rude Ralph.

'Oooh,' said Henry.

Ralph pulled two hideous skull heads from the bag. They had big empty eye sockets, and scary wisps of long straggly blonde and brown hair. They looked—they looked absolutely marvellous.

'Wow,' said Henry. 'Wow.' He reached out and touched the gruesome skulls.

He wanted those heads more than anything in the world.

'Where'd you get them?'

'Present from my gran,' said Ralph. 'These two are for you.'

'Thanks, Ralph,' said Henry.

Did anyone ever have a better friend than Ralph?

'This one looks like Margaret,' said Horrid Henry, swinging one of the heads by its pony tail.

'Just better-looking,' said Ralph rudely.

Henry and Ralph hung up the heads from the ceiling light. Yeah! The heads looked really horrible. Horrid Henry shivered.

Ralph grabbed hold of Henry's metal headband from his Evil Scientist Robot Kit and shoved it on top of his hair.

'Oooh, aaaahhh, eeeee, my head is shrinking . . .' yelped Ralph, writhing in his chair and laughing.

Horrid Henry stared at Ralph. He'd just had the most brilliant idea ever in the history of the universe.

If he could make Peter believe he could shrink heads, Peter would be in his power. He could make Peter give him all his crisps. He could get Peter's pocket money. He'd never have to steal Peter's chips again . . . Peter would just hand them over . . . or else. He would rule the house as King Henry the Horrible . . . forever.

'Peter!' bellowed Henry. 'Come quick. I have a present for you.'

Perfect Peter poked his head round the door.

'What?' said Peter.

'Who do you want?' asked Henry. 'Margaret or Susan?'

Huh?

'Up there,' said Horrid Henry, pointing.

Perfect Peter stared at the skulls dangling from the ceiling lamp. One had a dark pony tail. The other had a few blonde tufts.

'What are they?' said Peter cautiously.

'Margaret and Susan,' said Horrid Henry. 'They've annoyed me for the very last time. I shrank their heads.'

'Shame you missed it,' said Ralph.

Perfect Peter stared up at the shrunken heads.

No way. Absolutely no way.

'I don't believe you,' said Peter. He took a step back.

'I know an ancient cannibal curse,' said Henry. 'From my top secret curse book. When I say the curse, with the help of my trusty head-shrinker—pow!'

Perfect Peter recoiled.

He knew Henry was lying.

Henry had to be lying.

Henry couldn't really shrink heads . . . could he?

'You're lying,' said Peter.

'I'll prove it,' said Henry. 'If you're so sure I'm lying, then put on the head-shrinker and we'll find out.' He held up the metal headband. 'All you have to lose is your head.'

'NOOO!' said Peter.

'Why not?' said Horrid Henry. 'You'll be famous. You'll be helping science. I can't believe you don't want to take part in this experiment. You'll change history, Peter. Headless statues will be raised to you everywhere.'

Oooh, thought Peter. A headless statue of me. Wait a minute . . .

'I don't want to be a shrunken head,' said Peter. He edged away towards the door.

Rude Ralph stepped forward.

'I'll volunteer,' he said.

'Are you sure?' said Henry.

'Yes,' said Ralph. 'You need proof of your great invention. Just . . . just call it, The Ralph.'

'I promise,' said Horrid Henry. 'Thank you, Ralph. It's been great knowing you.'

Henry placed the metal shrinker over Ralph's head.

Perfect Peter watched, horrified, as Henry slowly tightened the screws.

'And now I will begin the head-shrink curse,' said Horrid Henry. He bowed his head and raised his arms to the ceiling.

'Oh, mighty head-shrinkers from the past,

Oonga Noonu and Aladocious Mimocious,

Gather round and have a blast . . .'

Rude Ralph began to shudder and shake. Henry carried on.

'You have your flesh, oh Oonga,
You have your power, oh Aladocious,
You have your magic, oh spirits.
Take this head, squeeze it tight,
Kooka boo kooka boo kooka boo—'

Rude Ralph gave a blood-curdling scream.

Perfect Peter yelped and ran out of the room.

'Mum! Help!!' wailed Peter, running downstairs. 'Henry is shrinking Ralph's head!'

Henry and Ralph choked with laughter.

'Henry. Get down here this minute,' shouted Mum. 'You horrid boy.'

Horrid Henry rolled his eyes.

'I'll be right back,' he said to Ralph, heading downstairs.

'Henry said he'd shrunk Margaret and Susan's heads,' whimpered Peter.

'And now he's shrinking Ralph's . . .'

'Henry, that was a horrible trick to play on Peter,' said Mum.

'It wasn't a trick,' said Henry. 'I was just doing a science experiment.'

'Henry, why can't you play nicely with your brother?' said Mum.

'I was playing nicely,' said Henry. 'I even offered to give Peter one of my shrunken heads as a present.'

And then Horrid Henry heard a piercing voice coming from next door's garden.

'It's hard being the most popular girl in the class. Everyone wants to be my friend,' brayed Moody Margaret.

'You aren't the most popular girl,' yelled Susan sourly. 'Everyone thinks you're a mean old bossy boots.'

Perfect Peter gasped.

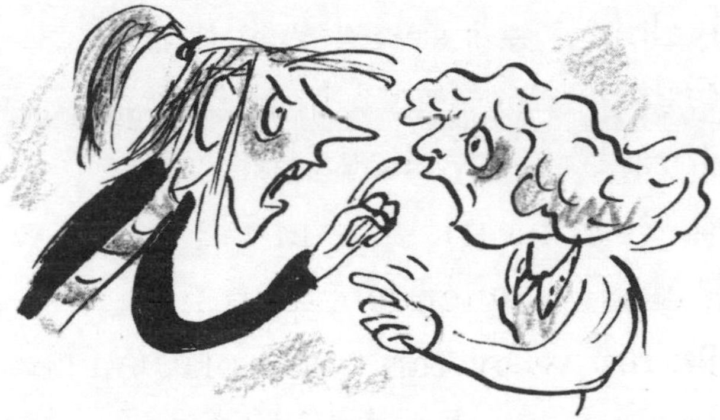

'You said you'd shrunk their heads,' he said. 'You lied.'

'I did shrink their heads,' said Henry. 'And then I unshrunk them.'

Mum sighed.

'Henry, I want you to leave Peter alone.'

Horrid Henry stared at his feet.

'Yes, Mum.'

Tra la la.

He'd got off lightly, thanks to his weasel words.

Henry dashed back upstairs and burst into his bedroom.

'Ralph! I got away with it. No punishment for me.'

Horrid Henry looked around.

No Ralph.

'Ralph?' said Henry.

On the chair where Ralph had been sitting was the headshrinker.

Inside the shrinker was . . . a shrunken head.

Ralph had vanished.

'Ralph?' said Henry.

That was odd.

'Ralph? You in the loo?'

Henry looked. No Ralph.

He checked under his bed.

No Ralph.

Slowly Horrid Henry approached the chair.

The skull had brown hair. Just like Ralph's.

'Ralph! Stop fooling around,' said Horrid Henry.

His heart began to pound.

Was Ralph—gone?

What had he done? What would he do?

'Nah na na nah nah,' yelped Ralph, leaping out of the wardrobe. 'Tricked you!'

AAAAAAARRRRGGGG-HHHHHHH!

Henry's Halloween Howlers

Who was the most famous skeleton detective?
Sherlock Bones

What's a monster's favourite soup?
Scream of tomato.

The police are looking for a monster with one eye.
Why don't they use two?

Who won the monster beauty contest?
No one.

What did one tomb say to another tomb?
Is that you, coffin?

What do devils drink?
Demonade

What time was it when the monster swallowed the Prime Minister?
Ate P.M.

What do you call a vampire who likes to relax in a bloodbath with a good book?
Well red.

HORRID HENRY'S SPOOKY FUN

CREEPY CRISS-CROSS

Can you fit these words into the criss-cross puzzle?

CLUE: Fill in the longest word first.

6 LETTERS
Zombie

7 LETTERS
Vampire
Monster

8 LETTERS
Werewolf

9 LETTERS
Hobgoblin

4 LETTERS
Ogre

5 LETTERS
Witch
Ghost
Troll

HORRiD HENRY'S HALLOWEEN FEEL BOX

Horrid Henry has a really horrible game for Halloween. If you want to make your friends and family scream, follow Henry's instructions.

• You will need a cardboard box – a large shoe box would be ideal. Cut a hole in the side of the box, large enough for a hand to fit through

• Put a selection of grisly items into the box, and tell people to feel inside and guess what's there

• If you're having a Halloween party, sit in a circle in the dark and pass the items round one by one. Tell your guests that you are passing around a dead witch's brain, then hand round a damp sponge! Do the same for each of the items

Here are a few ideas to get you started:
Dead witch's brains – damp sponge
Heart – hardboiled egg
Dried-up tongue – dried apricots
Veins – cold spaghetti
Eyeballs – peeled grapes or pearl onions
Skin – tortilla
Fingers – chipolatas
Ear – large mushroom

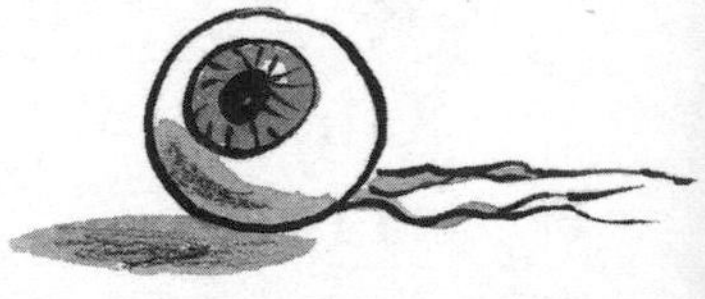

BODY SEARCH

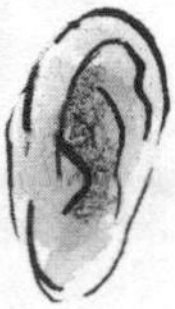

Find these body parts
in the wordsearch below.

EAR	NOSE	LIVER	TONGUE
NAIL	TEETH	MUSCLE	KIDNEY
VEIN	HEART	ARTERY	EYEBALL

K	N	E	P	N	T	D	Y
R	I	Z	L	E	A	R	X
E	E	D	E	C	E	I	N
V	V	T	N	T	S	O	L
I	H	Z	R	E	S	U	P
L	L	A	B	E	Y	E	M
W	U	T	O	N	G	U	E
D	T	R	A	E	H	D	X

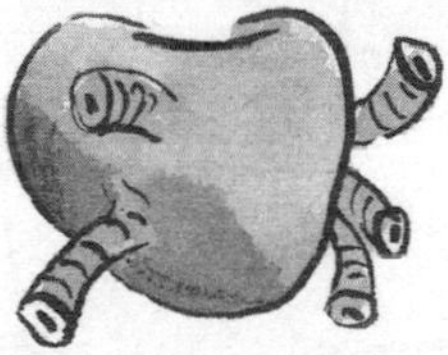

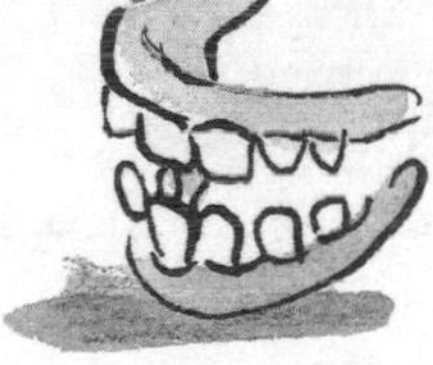

HORRID HENRY'S HALLOWEEN TOP TIPS

Horrid Henry loves Halloween! A day when you're supposed to stuff your face with sweets and play horrid tricks. Here are his top tips for the perfect trick or treat experience.

TRICK-OR-TREAT CHECKLIST

Most important of all is a huge bag to collect all your treats

A brilliant scary costume (see right)

A great bag of tricks

MAKE SURE YOU GET PROPER TREATS

Chocolate Hairballs

Belcher Squelchers

Spiky Spiders

~~Apples~~

~~Satsumas~~

~~Walnuts~~

WEAR A COOL AND SCARY COSTUME

Red-and-black devil

Mummy

Vampire

Zombie

~~Pink polka dot bunny~~

PRACTISE AN EVIL LAUGH – *HEH HEH HEH!*

DON'T TAKE YOUR LITTLE BROTHER OR SISTER – especially if they look really stupid. If they really, really have to go with you, lend them a costume.

Perfect Peter's TOP TIPS

- Smile sweetly
- Be polite and not too scary

MAKE A GHOULISH GHOST

You will need:
An old white bed sheet
Tracing paper
Pencil
Black fabric paint

Instructions:

1. Trace the templates of the ghostly eyes, nose and mouth.
2. Cut out your tracings.
3. Try on the sheet and work out the best positions for the eyes, nose and mouth.
4. Draw around your tracings to transfer the eyes, nose and mouth onto the sheet.
5. Paint using the fabric paint.
6. Cut out eyeholes to make sure you can see where you're going!
7. If you can't use a sheet, you could make a ghost mask, using a pillowcase instead.

SCARY DOT-TO-DOT

Join the dots to discover a scary surprise! (Hint: Rabid Rebecca hates these creepy crawlies . . .)

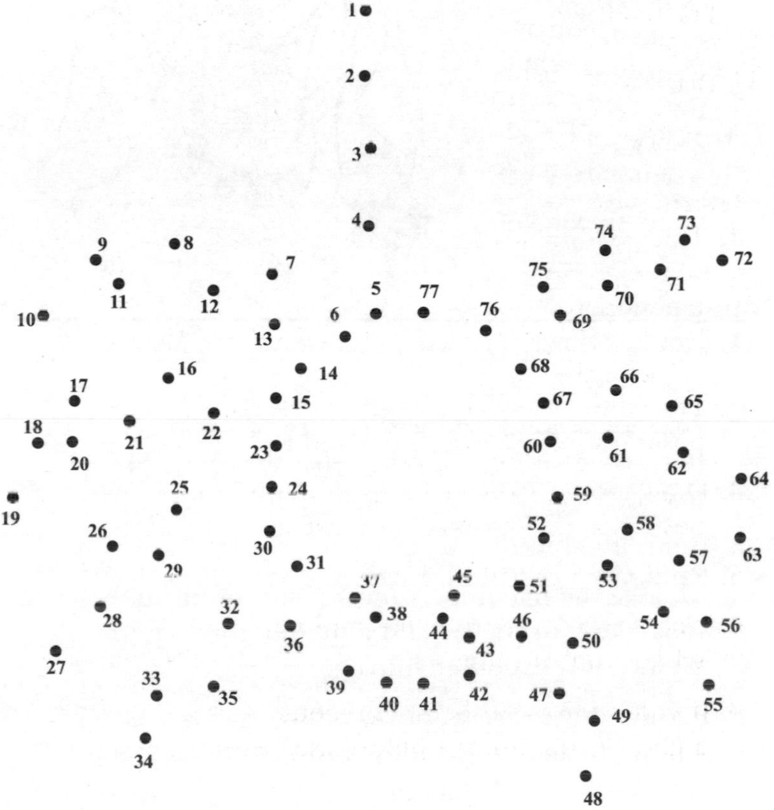

GREEDY GRAHAM'S GRiSLY GRUB

You will need:
3 cooked sausages
Tomato ketchup
Butter or margarine
2 slices of bread
5 almonds, halved or sliced

Instructions:

1. Cut the sausages in half lengthways – these are your fingers.
2. Poke an almond half or slice into one end of five of the sausage halves so that they look like fingernails.
3. Butter the bread.
4. Arrange the five fingers on the slice of bread to look like four fingers and a thumb, then squirt on lots of tomato ketchup.
5. Put the other slice of bread on top to make a sandwich, and press it down so that the ketchup (or blood!) oozes out.

You will need:
Celery
Red food colouring
Jug of water

Instructions:

1. Mix a few drops of food colouring with the water.
2. Cut the bottom off the celery and place it in the water.
3. Wait overnight. In the morning the celery will be stripy and look like it is soaked in blood!

You will need:
Marshmallows
Chocolate chips
Red icing tube

Instructions:

1. Push a chocolate chip in the middle of each of the marshmallows.
2. Using the red icing, draw blood vessels around the chocolate chip to make it look like an eye.

MOODY MARGARET'S FAKE BLOOD

Fake blood is fantastic! Try Moody Margaret's realistically revolting recipe.

You will need:
Golden syrup
Red food colouring
Cocoa powder
Water
Corn flour
A bowl or jar

Instructions:

1. Mix a couple of spoonfuls of golden syrup with red food colouring until it's the colour of blood.
2. Add a pinch of cocoa powder to darken the mixture, and make it look more like real blood.
3. If your blood is too thick, add a bit of water. If it's too thin, add a pinch of corn flour and mix it in slowly and carefully.
4. Then it's time to scare your family and friends … Dribble this fake blood from your mouth – it's OK to eat!

WEIRD WORDSEARCH

Can you find these nightmare names in the wordsearch puzzle below? Search up, down, left, right and diagonally.

POLTERGEIST	ZOMBIE	PHANTOM
GHOST	MONSTER	SKELETON
SPOOK	ALIEN	MUMMY

T	Z	Y	V	E	S	J	R	C	G	J
H	S	B	M	P	R	E	Q	C	N	W
P	Y	I	O	M	T	J	A	O	O	F
I	V	O	E	S	U	G	W	G	T	H
L	K	F	N	G	Z	M	I	H	E	T
L	B	O	Z	B	R	W	M	O	L	C
W	M	Q	P	O	S	E	K	S	E	L
M	N	X	H	U	M	Y	T	T	K	M
G	K	E	X	U	L	B	H	L	S	G
N	E	I	L	A	X	X	I	U	O	K
P	H	A	N	T	O	M	Y	E	M	P

BRAINY BRIAN'S MOVIE MONSTER QUIZ

Brainy Brian loves watching monster movies and he knows lots of film facts. Find out how much you know in this fun quiz.

1. **King Kong is discovered in a tropical forest. What is this giant movie monster?**

(a) A giant gorilla.
(b) A massive man-eating mouse.
(c) A super-sized snake.

2. **Dr Frankenstein created his famous movie monster from parts of other people and animals. What is special about the Monster's neck?**

(a) The Monster always wears a stripy scarf tied round it.
(b) It has a big bolt sticking all the way through it.
(c) Its wrapped up in a bandage.

3. **Which was the most monstrous dinosaur in 'Jurassic Park'?**

(a) Stegosaurus.
(b) Brachiosaurus.
(c) Tyrannosaurus Rex.

4. **The movie 'Jaws' stars a deadly sea monster. What is Jaws?**

(a) A jellyfish.
(b) A shark.
(c) A whale.

5. Count Dracula is a famous vampire who appears in lots of films. How is Dracula killed?

(a) He drowns in the sea.
(b) He falls out of a high window.
(c) Someone sticks a stake through his heart.

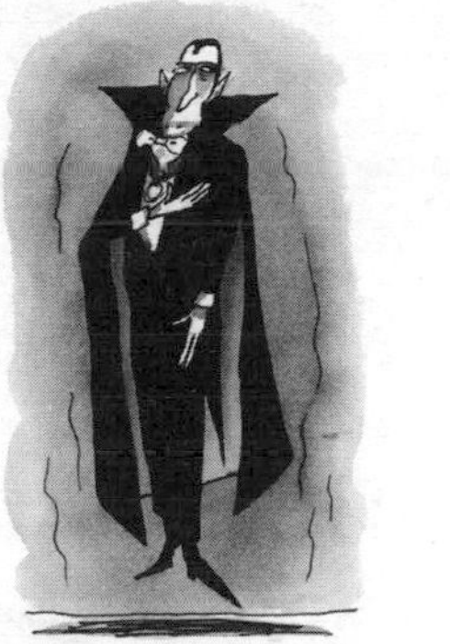

6. In the movie, 'Pirates of the Caribbean', there's a terrifying monster called the Kraken. What is it?

(a) A giant octopus.
(b) A bone-crunching crab.
(c) Man-eating seaweed.

7. In the Disney movie of Hercules, the hero chops off the horrific Hydra's head. But what happens next?

(a) The Hydra's head attacks Hercules.
(b) The Hydra grows another hundred heads.
(c) Hercules chops off the Hydra's tail.

8. The big, blue monster, Sulley, is from which movie?

(a) Shrek.
(b) Monster House.
(c) Monsters, Inc..

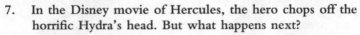

Flick to page 209 for the answers. How did you do?

6-8 Amazing! This mega-monstrous score proves that you're a movie monster boffin, just like Brainy Brian.

3-5 Not a totally terrible score – but you could definitely do better! Pester your parents like Horrid Henry does, and make sure you get to see all the scariest monster movies.

0-2 You're such a scaredy-pants! Like Perfect Peter, whenever there's a monster movie on TV, you're probably hiding terrified behind the sofa!

EVIL ENEMIES

It's Halloween and Horrid Henry is Trick or Treating. He sees a scary silhouette in the window. Can you recognise Henry's enemies from these shadowy shapes?

Write your answers below:

A ____________________

B ____________________

C ____________________

D ____________________

E ____________________

F ____________________

G ____________________

MONSTER MAZE

Help Perfect Peter through the maze – without meeting a monster!

SPOOKY SPIDERS

You will need:
A lot of black wool
A large-eyed needle
Scissors
4 pipe-cleaners
Cardboard
Glue
Googly eyes (or you can make your own out of paper)

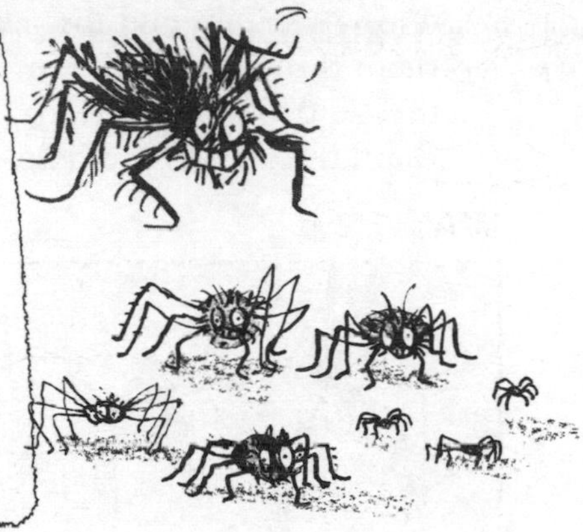

Instructions:

1. Cut out 2 cardboard circles, about 5 ½ cm in diameter, with a hole in the centre of each, about 2 ½ cm in diameter.

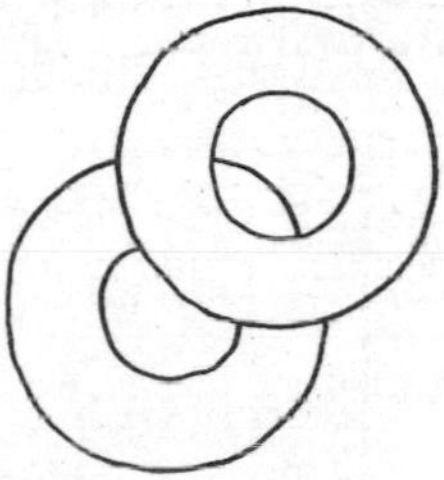

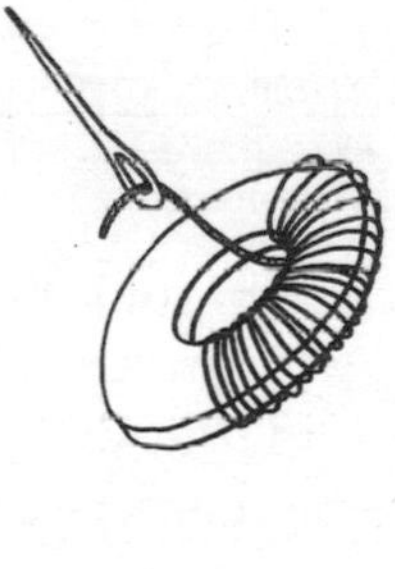

2. Thread the needle with the wool. Hold the 2 cardboard circles together and pass the needle through the centre hole and over the outside edge, over and over again until the circle is covered. Don't pull the wool tight.

3. When you have finished winding the wool, take the 4 pipe-cleaners and thread them through the hole in the centre of the cardboard. Bend them in the middle.

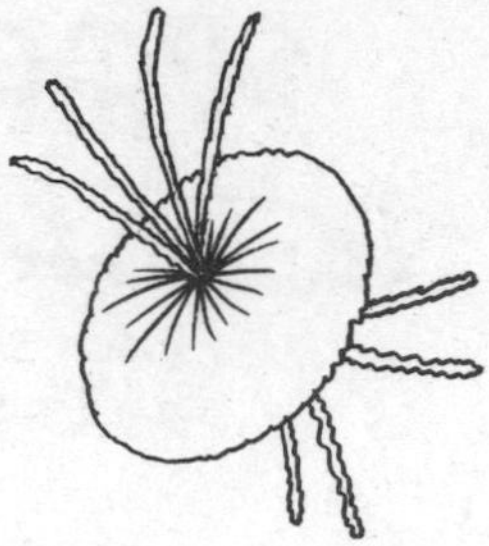

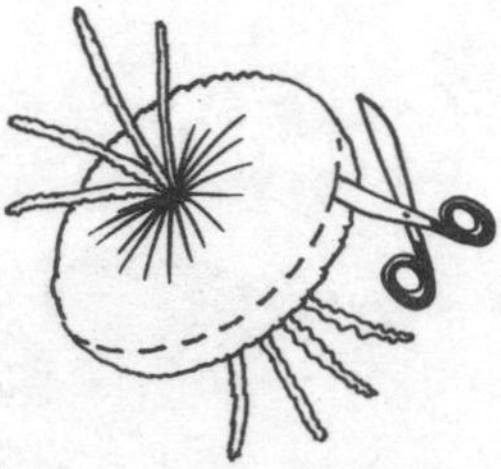

4. Now cut the wool between the edges of the 2 cardboard circles.

5. Double up a long length of wool. Slip it between the cardboard cirles and tie it very tightly.

6. Carefully remove the cardboard circles.

7. Bend the spider's pipe-cleaner legs and stick on the eyes. Use the long piece of wool tied around the centre to hang the spider up in dark, gloomy corners.

WHAT DO YOUR NIGHTMARES REVEAL ABOUT YOU?

1. **If your favourite dream turned into a nightmare, which one of these three options would it be?**

(a) You've just won loads of cold hard cash and you can't wait to spend it all – then your parents put it all in the bank to save until you are grown up.
(b) You're the Prime Minister and everyone obeys you – but then your best friend becomes Prime Minister instead and throws you into jail.
(c) You're walking through a meadow of lovely flowers with your mum, but when you pick a bunch of flowers for her, she gets cross and tells you off.

2. **In your nightmare, you are being chased – but who is chasing you?**

(a) A very angry teacher.
(b) A mean best friend you don't like any more.
(c) A scary pirate who chops people's heads off.

3. **You are having a nightmare about school. Which of these is most likely?**

(a) Your horrible teacher has given you hours and hours of homework.
(b) You aren't captain of the school football team any more – in fact, you're not even on the team.
(c) You haven't got any gold stars in the Good as Gold book.

4. **You are all alone in a nightmarish place. Where is it?**

(a) In a muddy field in the countryside, surrounded by fierce bulls.
(b) In your enemies' den, with no one to boss around.
(c) In a very noisy, brightly-lit restaurant, like Gobble and Go.

5. **A ghost is haunting your dreams. What is it like?**

(a) A great big spooky bunny with no tail and huge teeth coming to get you.
(b) A screeching ghoul with blood dripping from its mouth.
(c) A misty graveyard ghost moaning and wailing.

6. **A monster is coming towards you in your nightmare. Is it . . .**

(a) A zombie vampire werewolf.
(b) A creepy acid alien.
(c) A hairy scary monster with big claws.

7. You're having the worst nightmare ever! What is it?

(a) Crisps, sweets and chocolate are banned – for the rest of your life.
(b) You never win at anything ever again.
(c) You've lost your favourite cuddly toy.

8. Your nightmare is so scary, it wakes you up. What do you do?

(a) Quickly hide under the covers.
(b) Scream very loudly, then go straight back to sleep.
(c) Run crying to Mum and Dad's room.

Count up how many (a)s, (b)s and (c)s you've chosen, then check below to see what your score reveals about you.

Mostly (a)s: Like Horrid Henry, you hate school, teachers and homework. You're secretly scared of spooks, vampires and zombies – but you're even more scared of losing all your pocket money and sweets.

Mostly (b)s: Like Moody Margaret, you love being in charge. You're a teeny-tiny bit scared of ghouls and aliens, but your biggest nightmare is being a loser and somebody else bossing you about!

Mostly (c)s: Like Perfect Peter, you want to be as good as gold. You're scared of monsters, ghosts and pirates – but you're even more terrified of being told off.

FANGMANGLER FUN

Answer the clues and fit the words into the crossword puzzle. Each word begins with one of the letters in the word FANGMANGLER.

Across

1. An old fashioned light.
3. A girl's name.
5. Something sharp, used for sewing.
9. Covered in oil or butter. Add to 3 across to make a demon dinner lady!
10. Spooks make this sound.
11. Works in a hospital. Add to 5 across to make someone who tries to give Horrid Henry an injection.

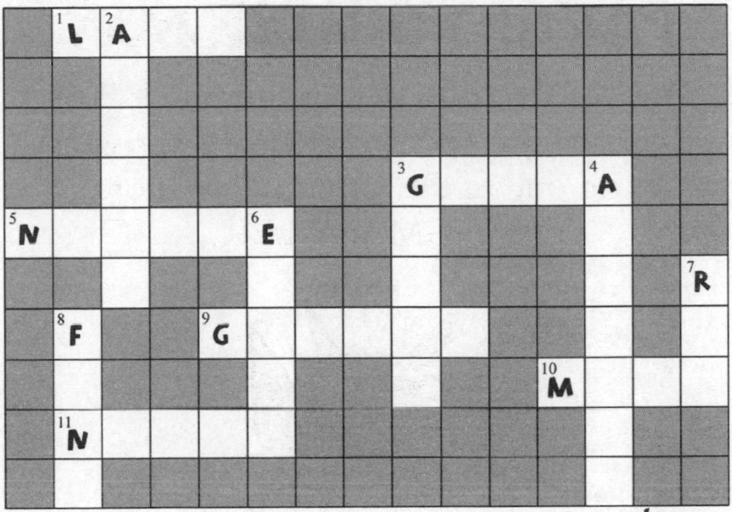

Down

2. A boy's name.
3. See-through and haunting.
4. Worried. Add to 2 down to make a nervous character in Henry's class.
6. Spooky and creepy.
7. The best thing to do if you see a Fangmangler!
8. A sharp tooth.

SCARY SHADOWS

Horrid Henry loves scaring Perfect Peter on Halloween with spooky shadows.

You will need:

Coloured pencils
Black card
Scissors
Straws
Sticky Tape
A torch

Instructions:

1. On the black card, draw the outline of something scary – like a big spider or a monster. You could copy Horrid Henry's monster (opposite) or create your own shape.
2. Cut your shape out carefully with scissors. Ask an adult to help you.
3. Stick a straw to your shape with sticky tape to make a handle.
4. Now find a room with a plain white or pale wall.
5. Turn off the light in the room, and get someone to shine the torch on the wall.
6. Move your scary spider or monster in the torch's light to make their ghostly shadows dance on the wall!

BIG SCARY PHOBIAS

WICCAPHOBIA (fear of witches) or PHASMORPHOBIA (fear of ghosts). Find more weird and wonderful phobias in the wordsearch – the words are in the box below.

L	C	A	E	V	L	A	O	C	Y	J	A	O	S
A	A	L	I	W	A	I	Y	Q	Y	I	S	M	O
I	I	C	I	B	D	B	J	T	B	Q	L	P	M
B	F	G	H	N	O	O	J	O	O	X	E	H	N
O	Y	J	O	A	O	H	H	N	E	X	H	A	I
H	E	Q	M	C	N	P	P	R	V	I	P	L	P
P	H	U	C	K	O	O	H	O	P	Y	K	O	H
O	L	A	F	N	I	I	P	O	T	V	R	P	O
S	F	S	O	P	O	L	Z	H	B	U	I	H	B
Y	E	G	Z	T	I	B	O	C	O	I	L	O	I
M	O	Z	B	D	X	I	U	E	U	B	A	B	A
P	K	I	R	V	U	B	Y	S	P	J	I	I	A
B	U	F	O	N	O	P	H	O	B	I	A	A	X
A	I	B	O	H	P	I	C	E	L	O	C	S	A

PHOBIA	FEAR OF ...	PHOBIA	FEAR OF ...
Ablutophobia	washing	Somniphobia	sleep
Bibliophobia	books	Bufonophobia	toads
Clinophobia	going to bed	Omphalophobia	belly buttons
Pogonophobia	beards	Scoleciphobia	worms
Lachanophobia	vegetables	Mysophobia	dirt

MONSTER SPOTTING

Here's Henry's very special guide to spotting terrifying zombie vampires . . .

How to recognise a vampire

1. Big huge scary teeth
2. Drinks blood
3. Only appears at night
4. Dark clothes
5. Can't see his or her reflection in the mirror
6. Mean and moody
7. Pale skin

How to recognise a zombie

1. Looks dead
2. Scary bulging eyes
3. Walks very slowly
4. Doesn't say a lot
5. Feeds on flesh
6. Bad hair

How to recognise a zombie-vampire

All of the above – but being half-zombie means they can walk about in daylight. Help!

SPOOKY SOUNDS

What sort of sound effects can you create using the things you find in your house?

Vampire Bats

Make a scary, flapping sound of vampire bats swooping to attack by opening and closing an umbrella very quickly.

Flesh-eating Zombies

Make the squishy sound of zombies feasting on flesh by chomping and slurping on a mouthful of chewy jelly sweets.

Bone Crunching

Put some dry pasta shells on a hard floor and stamp on the pasta to create the sound of bones crunching!

Vile Vomiting

Take two bowls of milk and cereal and let them go mushy. Pour one bowl into the other to make the sound of someone throwing up.

You're Being Followed

To create the creepy sound of someone walking behind you, hold two shoes, tap the heels together, and then tap the shoes.

Giant Man-eating Bugs

Make the sound of a buzzing insect by wrapping greaseproof paper tightly round a comb, then hum with your lips, just touching the paper.

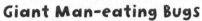

Rainstorm

Pour uncooked rice onto a metal baking sheet – lightly to create a drizzle or heavily for a full-on downpour!

COULD YOU SURVIVE A ZOMBIE INVASION?

1. Is it better to face zombies as a team or alone?

(a) Stick with your friends. The more of you there are, the better your chance of survival.
(b) Stay together and obey the leader.
(c) You've got more chance on your own, especially if your team-mates are really rubbish.

2. How do you decide on a plan of action?

(a) Talk about it with your team-mates and do something that everyone is happy with.
(b) The leader decides what you're going to do.
(c) Just turn up and see what happens.

3. A group of zombies have invaded the sweet shop, but you're hungry. What do you do?

(a) Run away – as far from the sweet shop as you can.
(b) Argue about what to do for so long that the zombies have gobbled up all the sweets and are coming after you!
(c) Hide outside the shop until you think the zombies have gone, then nip in and buy your sweets.

4. The zombies are coming to your school. What's your plan?

(a) Escape out the back door.
(b) Send Miss Battle-Axe to sort them out.
(c) Hide under your desk.

5. The zombies are shuffling towards your house. Where do you hide?

(a) In Moody Margaret's tree house – pulling up the ladder behind you.
(b) Behind the sofa.
(c) Under the duvet.

6. If a zombie catches you, what's the worse thing that can happen?

(a) It bites you, and you become a zombie too.
(b) It makes you hand over all of your pocket money.
(c) It wants to be in the Purple Hand Gang and be your best friend.

7. The zombies are battering down your front door. There's no escape – What do you do?

(a) Cover yourself in fake blood and pretend to be a zombie.
(b) Scream very loudly and tell them to GO AWAY.
(c) Give in and join them.

8. You manage to escape the zombie invasion and find a hideway. What have you brought with you?

(a) Water, food and blankets.
(b) A pirate hat and cutlass.
(c) A goo-shooter and some day-glo slime.

Count up how many (a)s, (b)s and (c)s you've got, then check your results below to reveal your ideal team and discover your chances of survival.

Mostly (a)s: Welcome to the winning team! The A-TEAM is Aerobic Al, Brainy Brian, Clever Clare and Tough Toby, combining speed, brains and toughness. Perfect for escaping and outwitting the zombies.

Mostly (b)s: Bad luck. You're on the B-TEAM, with Moody Margaret as team leader, plus Sour Susan, Gorgeous Gurinder and Singing Soraya. If you do everything Moody Margaret tells you, you'll be able to stay on the team and might even be promoted to Deputy Team Leader. But if you disagree with Margaret, you'll be thrown to the zombies!

Mostly (c)s: Like Horrid Henry, you're too cunning and clever to be on a team with a load of losers. Armed with a trusty goo-shooter and some day-glo slime, you're brave enough to go into battle alone against a million trillion zombies – SPLAT!

HOW TO HOLD A ZOMBiE PARTY

INVITATIONS

- Make invitations out of black card or paper.
- Write in white chalk or crayon when and where your party will be held.
- Don't invite any scaredy cats.
- Tell your friends to come dressed up as zombies.

- Decorate your invitations by drawing on eyeballs – or sticking on plastic googly eyes.

PARTY FOOD

Finger sandwiches
Edible Eyeballs
Blood Red jelly
Blackcurrant Juice

ZOMBIE MAKEOVERS

When your guests arrive, give them all a scary makeover with face paints.

ZOMBIE GAMES

Make a Zombie Giggle

Choose someone to be the Zombie IT – Zit for short. All the other players are zombies. They must lie quietly on the floor without moving. Zit has to try and make the zombies giggle – but he's not allowed to touch them! The last zombie left is the winner.

Pin the Eyeball on the Zombie

Draw or print out a large picture of a zombie, and a separate picture of an eyeball. Blindfold your friends in turn, spin them around and see who can pin the eyeball in the right place.

Hunt the Eyeball

Fill a large bowl with cooked spaghetti, and hide ping pong balls in it. Time how long it takes each of your friends to find the eyeballs.

Zombie Parade

Get all your party guest together for a zombie parade. Silently stagger around the house and garden, staring scarily ahead in a zombie-like fashion. See if you can frighten your parents or your little brothers and sisters.

TRiCKY TRiCKS

Horrid Henry and Rude Ralph know the best gruesome tricks to play on friends and family on Halloween.

VICIOUS VENOM

Make it look like a monster is spitting out deadly venom into its victim's eye. This is brilliant for scaring parents.

Props:
A garden hose
A helper, like Rude Ralph (or Perfect Peter if I'm desperate)

What I do:

1. Ralph hides in the garden with the garden hose.
2. I turn the water on so it sprays out of the hose, then start shouting 'HELP! THERE'S A MONSTER IN THE GARDEN!' so my parents come rushing out of the house.
3. From his hiding place, Ralph sprays the water at my face so that it looks like the monster is squirting venom in my eyes.
4. I scream more loudly, 'DEADLY VENOM! OUCH!' and roll around on the ground in pain, rubbing my eyes.

SEVERED HAND

Make it look as if a monster has ripped off your hand.

Props:

Wear a long-sleeved t-shirt
A rubber glove
Water
Cornflour
Red food colouring

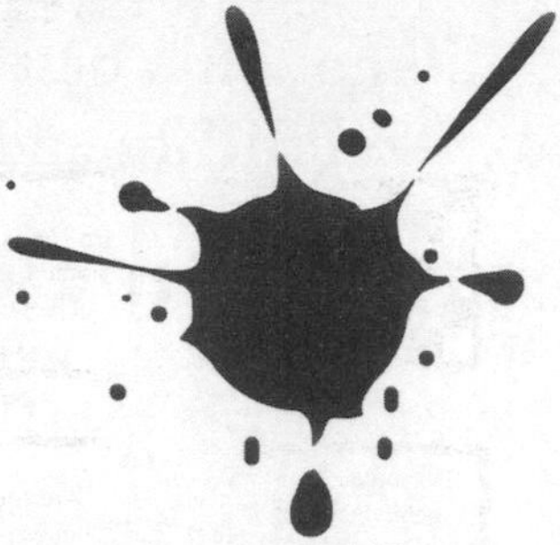

What I do:

1. I mix together water and cornflour until I get a thick paste.
2. Then I add enough red food colouring until the mixture looks like blood – bleech! – and put it in the rubber glove.
3. I hold the glove under one of my sleeves, then Ralph pulls my 'arm' off in front of Margaret and Susan. Blood pours everywhere and I howl in pain, and Margaret and Susan run away, screaming loudly. Ha!

HOW SCARED ARE YOU?

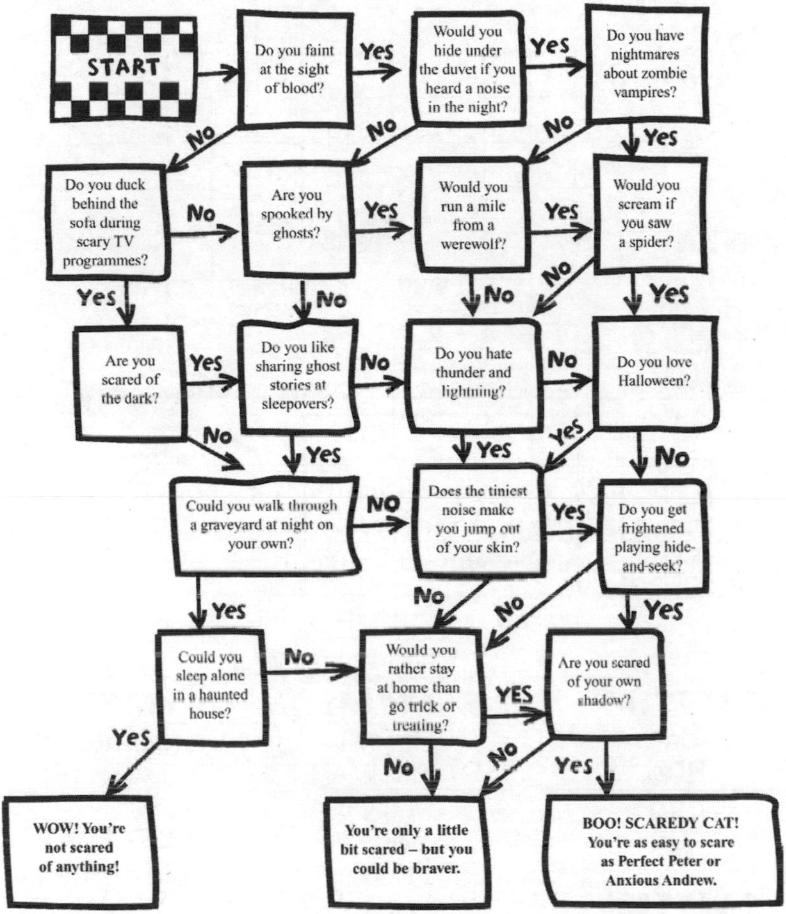

PUTRID PUZZLE

Can you solve the Halloween Puzzle below?

CLUE:
Fill in the 4 letter word first.

3 LETTERS
Bat
Boo
Fun
Web

4 LETTERS
Mask

5 LETTERS
Night
Party
Scary
Spook
Treat
Trick
Witch

6 LETTERS
Spider
Sweets

7 LETTERS
Costume
October
Pumpkin

POLTERGEIST PUZZLE

A sneaky poltergeist is up to mischief in Perfect Peter's tidy bedroom. Take a good look at Peter's room on the page BEFORE the poltergeist gets up to its tricks, then turn the page and see if you can spot 10 differences.

POLTERGEIST PUZZLE (PART 2)

Now look again. Can you circle the 10 differences without looking back at page 189?

MELTING MISS BATTLE-AXE

Henry loves to play games on Halloween, especially if he can get revenge on Miss Battle-Axe at the same time!

You will need:

A blackboard
Chalk – any colours
A sponge for each player
A bucket of water

What to do:

1. Draw a picture of Miss Battle-Axe on the blackboard using chalk.
2. Fill the bucket with water.
3. In turn, each player puts their sponge in the water, squeezes it out and throws it at the blackboard.
4. As Miss Battle-Axe gets wet, she starts looking as if she is melting.
5. When Henry's scary teacher has completely melted away, everyone is a winner!

HORRID HENRY'S GHOST GUIDE

Here are the ghostly ghouls you are likely to meet on a dark and spooky night. Remember all ghosts are terrified of the phrase, 'Be gone, worms!'

1. Graveyard ghouls

2. Alien acid monsters

3. Clanking headless knights

4. Great-aunts in rocking chairs

5. Margaret the frog ghost

6. Zombie mummies

7. Vampire chickens

8. Injection bunnies (scariest of all)

HORRID HENRY'S BRAIN-BURSTING QUIZ

1. **When Henry sneaks downstairs in the dark and lands on something lumpy on the comfy black chair, what does he do?**

(a) He quietly turns on the light to see what it is.
(b) He screams, 'AAARRRRGGGH!'
(c) He attacks the lumpy thing with a cushion.

2. **What is a Fangmangler?**

(a) The slimiest, scariest, most horrible and frightening monster in the whole world.
(b) The latest gadget for sale in Toy Heaven.
(c) Something Henry has made up to scare everyone.

3. **How does Henry try to make Peter look scarier on Halloween?**

(a) He gives him a scary haircut.
(b) He cuts off his little bunny tail.
(c) He makes him wear an evil mask.

4. Which of Peter's toys is Henry desperate to get his hands on?

(a) Bunnikins.
(b) Snoozie Whoozie, a bunny that giggles you to sleep.
(c) The Curse of the Mummy kit.

5. When Henry has a sleepover at New Nick's, what's the scariest thing that happens to Henry in the night?

(a) Nick's little sister, Lisping Lily, tries to kiss him.
(b) Five wet smelly dogs pounce on him.
(c) The wind howls through the bedroom window.

6. When Henry stays at Aunt Ruby's, he hears a ghostly noise from the wardrobe in the night. What does he do?

(a) He runs crying to Aunt Ruby's room.
(b) He grabs his goo-shooter, gets out of bed and flings open the wardrobe door.
(c) He hides under the duvet.

7. What does Henry do to try and get out of an injection?

(a) He runs away.
(b) He pretends to be ill.
(c) He kicks Nurse Needle.

8. At Perfect Peter's pirate party, Henry invents a pirate to scare Peter. What's he called?

(a) Sammy the Shrunken Head Slug.
(b) The Purple Hand Pirate.
(c) Blood Boil Bob, the Cannibal Pirate.

Don't be scared!

Turn to page 213 to find out the answers.

6–8: A sizzling score.
Your knowledge is spine-tingling!

3–5: You know some fiendish facts, but not enough to be totally terrifying.

1–2: AAAAGH! Your score is so low – it's scary!

ANXIOUS ANDREW'S WORRIED WORDSEARCH

Anxious Andrew doesn't like Halloween – it's far too worrying! Find all the things that make Andrew anxious on Halloween in the below wordsearch.

S	W	I	T	C	H	E	S
N	S	V	T	O	Y	R	P
I	K	E	F	X	E	M	O
K	S	F	N	D	J	S	O
P	A	U	I	K	T	A	K
M	M	P	G	A	R	J	S
U	S	M	B	Z	N	A	N
P	S	T	S	O	H	G	D

SPIDERS	DARKNESS
SPOOKS	MASKS
WITCHES	BATS
GHOSTS	PUMPKINS

MONSTER MiSSING WORDS

Fit the words below into the criss-cross puzzle. Then use them to complete the punchlines for the monster jokes on the next page.

CLUE:
Put in the two longest words first.

3 LETTERS

Out
Sun

6 LETTERS

Ribbon
Waiter

4 LETTERS

Miss
Nose
Hide
Shop
Back

What happens if a big, hairy monster sits in front of you at the cinema?
You _ _ _ _ most of the movie.

What do you get if a huge monster steps on Batman and Robin?
Flatman and _ _ _ _ _ _ _.

What will a monster eat in a restaurant?
The _ _ _ _ _ _ _.

How do you know when there's a monster under your bed?
Your _ _ _ _ touches the ceiling.

What do you do with a green monster?
Put it in the _ _ _ until it ripens.

Why did the monster paint himself in rainbow colours?
Because he wanted to _ _ _ _ in the crayon box.

Where did the big, hairy monster go when he lost a hand?
He went to the second-hand _ _ _ _.

What should you do if a monster runs through your front door?
Run through the _ _ _ _ door.

Why did the monster have to buy two tickets for the zoo?
One to get in and one to get _ _ _.

MOODY MARGARET'S SCREAMING BANSHEE BALLOON

Moody Margaret loves scaring people on Halloween with her ear piercing screaming balloon.

You will need:
A balloon
A plastic straw
Rubber band
Scissors

Instructions:

1. Cut a 4cm piece from the plastic straw.
2. Push the straw inside the tube of the balloon. Leave 2cm sticking out of the end.
3. Wrap the rubber band around the straw and the balloon, so the straw is securely fixed inside the balloon.
4. Blow the balloon up through the straw, then hold the straw tightly so the air doesn't escape.
5. Let go of the straw - and hold your hands over your ears!

WOULD YOU MAKE A GOOD GHOST HUNTER?

Have you got what it takes to hunt ghosts? Follow the arrows to find out!

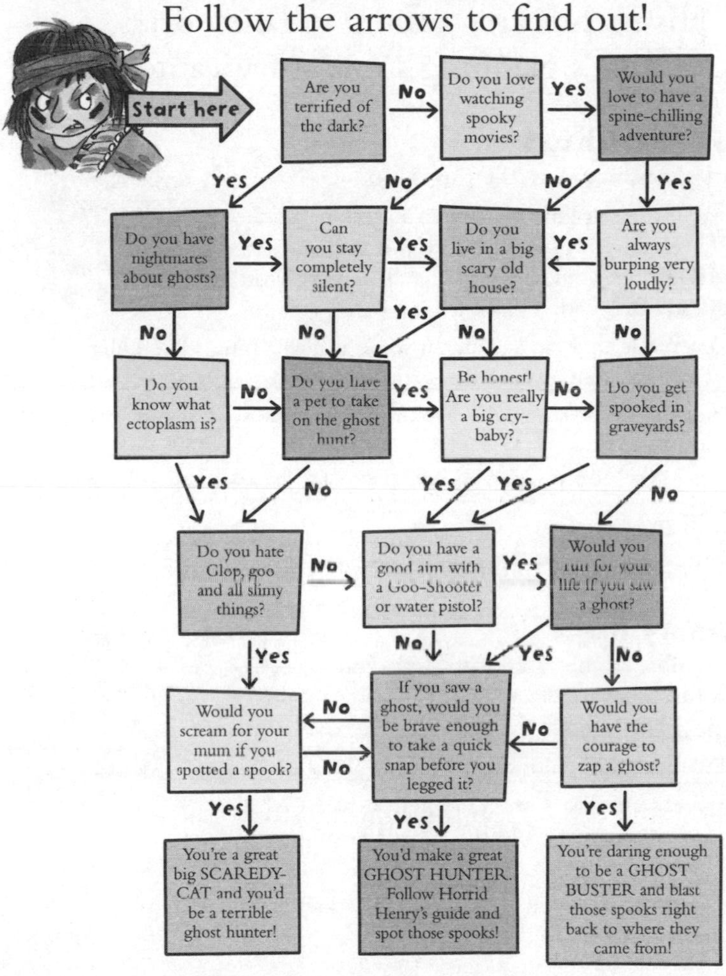

SPINE-TINGLING SLEEPOVER

Horrid Henry is having a spooky sleepover. His friends are coming in fancy dress, and he's planning some scary games.

Pass the Ghost

Henry's version of pass the parcel.

- Sneak into your little brother's room, pinch one of his clean, white socks and stuff it with sweets. Fasten the end with a rubber band, and draw on a ghostly face with a black felt-tip pen.
- Sit everyone in a circle, put on some brilliant music like killer boy rats and pass around the sock.
- When the music stops, the person holding the sock is out of the game.
- When there's only 1 person left, they win the sock and all the sweets.
- If your little brother wins, tell him he's won his sock, and has to share all of the sweets. That's the rule. Ha ha!

Mummy Race

The purpose of the game is to wrap your partner in toilet paper as fast as possible.

- Grab all the toilet paper from the bathroom when your mum's not looking.
- Put everyone into pairs. One person has to do the wrapping and the other person has to be mummified alive.
- The team with the first person to be completely covered is the winner.

Pin on the Nose

A monstrous version of pin the tail on the donkey.

- On a big piece of paper or cardboard, draw the scariest creature you can think of – a witch or a monster or, even scarier, Miss Battle-Axe! Draw in their eyes and mouth, but put a large X where the nose should be.
- On separate pieces of paper, draw as many noses as you will need, and put some sticky tape or fixers on the back of each one.

- Blindfold each person in turn and give them a nose.
- Spin the person round a few times. Stop them when they're facing the picture. They have to try and stick the nose in the right place.
- When everyone's had a go, the person with the nose closest to the X is the winner.

Murder in the Dark

A brilliant game for scaring big babies like Perfect Peter.

- Make enough slips of paper for all your guests. On one of them write 'murderer', on another write 'detective' and on all the rest write 'suspect'. Fold them up to hide the writing.
- Put the slips in a bowl and let everyone pick one.

- Don't tell anyone else what you are, unless you are the detective.
- If you are the detective, go and wait outside the room, turning off the light as you go.
- Now the fun starts. In the dark, the murderer chooses a victim and taps that person on the shoulder. The victim falls to the ground.
- When someone stumbles over the 'body', he shouts, 'Murder in the Dark'.
- The detective returns to the scene of the crime, turns the light back on – and tries to guess who committed the murder.

HORRID HENRY'S TOP TEN SCARY MOMENTS

10 The day I was forced to go on a walk in the countryside by my mean, horrible parents and nearly got gobbled by goats.

9 When Aunt Ruby took us to eat in Restaurant Le Posh – no burgers, no chips, no pizza. Just strange, horrible food in a gloopy sauce. Yuck!

8 When my horrid wormy-worm brother made everyone think I wanted to marry Moody Margaret. I'd rather marry Miss Battle-Axe than marry Margaret.

7 In the haunted house, when I heard spooky sounds coming from the wardrobe.

6 I agreed to eat all my vegetables for FIVE nights in a row, so my horrible parents would take me to Gobble and Go. But when the great day finally arrived, Gobble and Go wasn't there any more!

5 Staying overnight in Our Town Museum, when a creepy monster grabbed my leg in the dark.

4 When I, Horrid Henry, wore frilly pink lacy girls' pants covered in hearts and bows to school – and the latest craze in the playground was debagging. Horror of horrors!

3 The night the slimiest, scariest, most horrible and frightening monster in the whole world, the Fangmangler, leapt out of the bushes with a thunderous roar.

2 The day Nurse Needle tried to give me an injection with the longest, sharpest, most wicked needle I'd ever seen.

1 Horrible, horrible Thursday! The class swimming day when I was the only one left alone in the swimming pool – with a shark.

Goodbye, gruesome gang!

ANSWERS

p.151

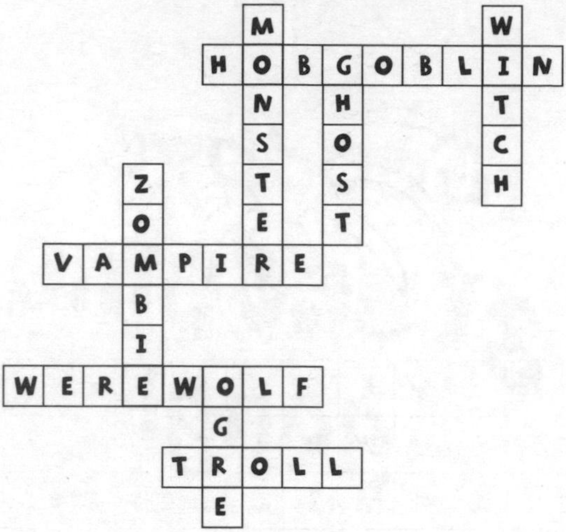

p.153

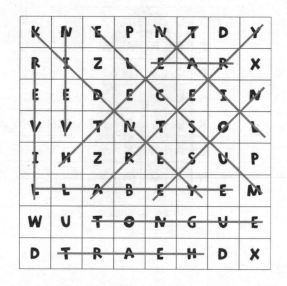

K	N	E	P	N	T	D	Y
R	I	Z	L	E	A	R	X
E	E	D	E	C	E	I	N
V	V	T	N	T	S	O	L
I	H	Z	R	E	S	U	P
L	L	A	B	E	Y	E	M
W	U	T	O	N	G	U	E
D	T	R	A	E	H	D	X

p.157

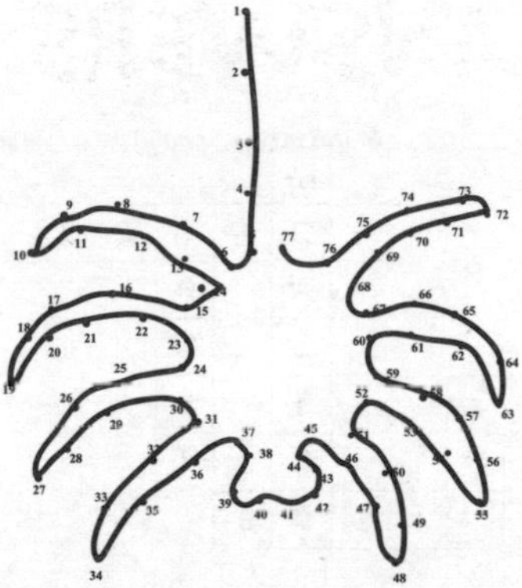

p.161

T	Z	Y	V	E	S	J	R	C	G	J
H	S	B	M	P	R	E	Q	C	N	W
P	Y	I	O	M	T	J	A	O	O	F
I	V	O	E	S	U	G	W	G	T	H
L	K	F	N	G	Z	M	I	H	E	T
L	B	O	Z	B	R	W	M	O	L	C
W	M	Q	P	O	S	E	K	S	E	L
M	N	X	H	U	M	Y	T	T	K	M
G	K	E	X	U	L	B	H	L	S	G
N	E	I	L	A	X	X	I	U	O	K
P	H	A	N	T	O	M	Y	E	M	P

p.162-163

1. (a)
2. (b)
3. (c)
4. (b)
5. (c)
6. (a)
7. (b)
8. (c)

p.164-165

A. Miss Battle-Axe
B. Rabid Rebecca
C. Moody Margaret
D. Bossy Bob
E. Greasy Greta
F. Miss Impatience Tutu
G. Sour Susan

p.166

p.172-173

	1 L	2 A	M	P										
		N												
		D												
		R						3 G	R	E	T	4 A		
5 N	E	E	D	L	6 E			H				N		
		W			E			O				X		7 R
	8 F			9 G	R	E	A	S	Y			I		U
	A				I			T			10 M	O	A	N
	11 N	U	R	S	E							U		
	G											S		

p.176

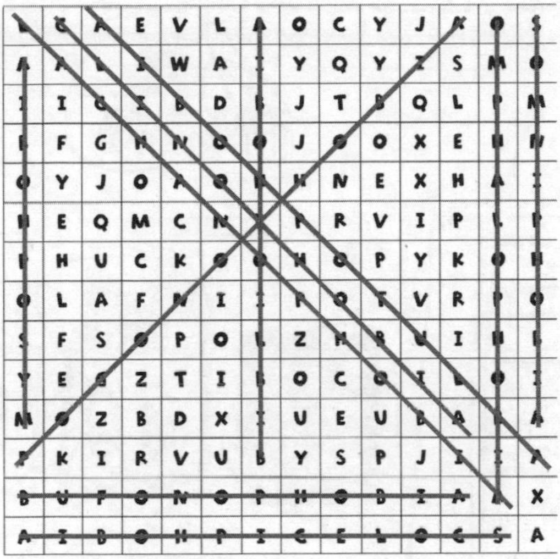

p.188

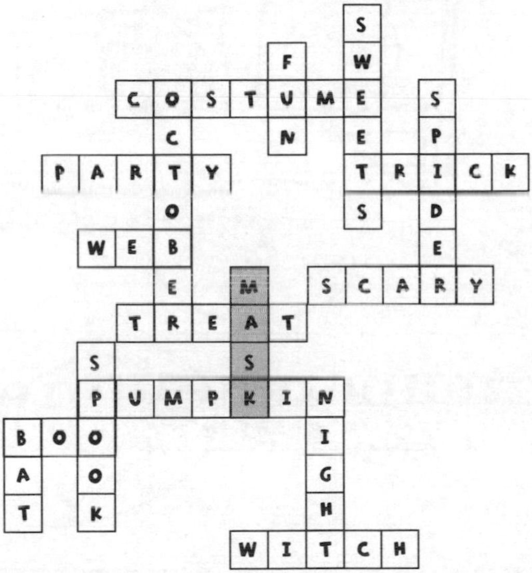
COSTUME
FUN
SWEETS
SPIDER
OCTOBER
PARTY
TRICK
WEB
SCARY
TREAT
MASK
SPOOK
PUMPKIN
BOO
BAT
NIGHT
WITCH

p.189–190

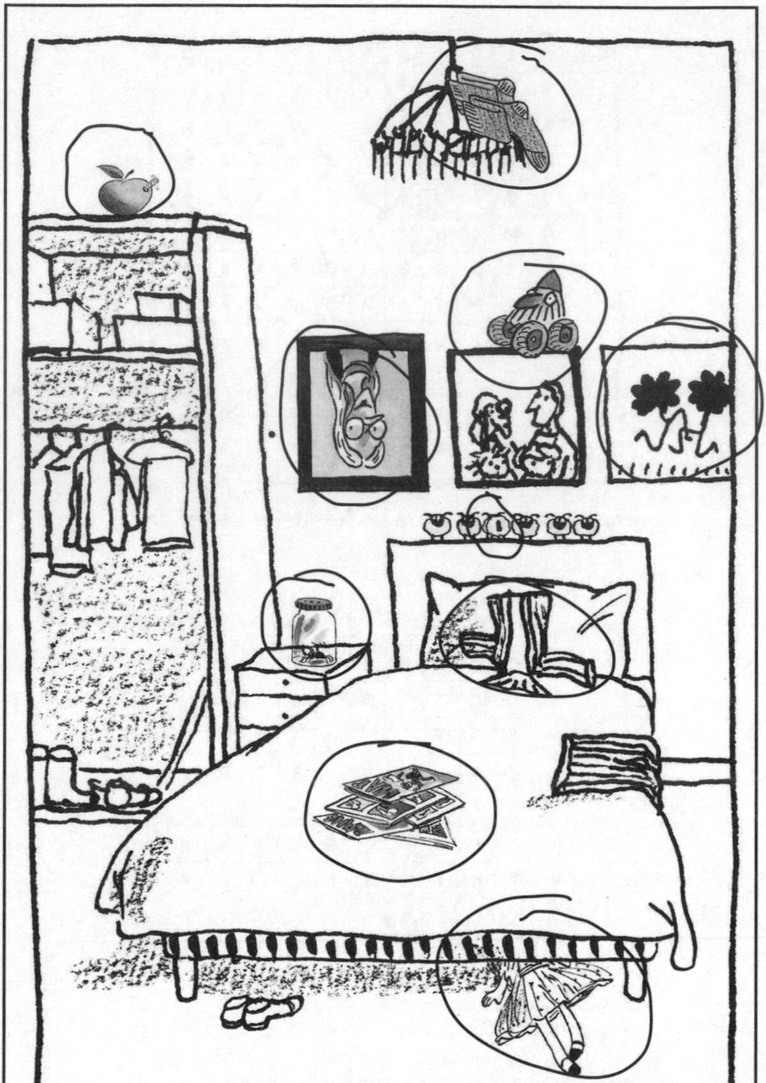

p.194-196

1. (b)	3. (a)	5. (a)	7. (b)
2. (c)	4. (c)	6. (b)	8. (c)

p.197

S	W	I	T	C	H	E	S
N	S	V	T	O	Y	R	P
I	K	E	F	X	E	M	O
K	S	F	N	D	J	S	O
P	A	U	I	K	T	A	K
M	M	P	G	A	R	J	S
U	S	M	B	Z	N	A	N
P	S	T	S	O	H	G	D

p.198-199

1. Miss	4. Nose	7. Shop
2. Ribbon	5. Sun	8. Back
3. Waiter	6. Hide	9. Out

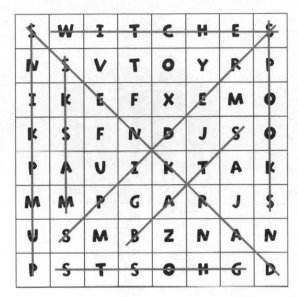

WHERE'S HORRID HENRY?

Featuring 32 pages of fiendish things to spot, join Henry and his friends (and evilest enemies!) on their awesome adventures – from birthday parties and camping trips to hiding out at a spooky haunted house. With a challenging checklist of things to find, this is Henry's most horrid challenge yet!

The question is, where's Horrid Henry?

WHERE'S HORRID HENRY COLOURING BOOK

A fun-packed Horrid Henry colouring book, filled with pages of Horrid Henry chaos to colour in. Turn Miss Battle-Axe's hair blue, give Moody Margaret a makeover, or make Perfect Peter look like the worm he really is!

Get creative with Horrid Henry!

Visit Horrid Henry's website at
www.horridhenry.co.uk for competitions,
games, downloads and a monthly newsletter